Tenorman

Tenorman

A NOVELLA BY DAVID HUDDLE

CHRONICLE BOOKS
SAN FRANCISCO

Printed in the United States of America.

Library of Congress Cataloging-in-Publication Data:
Huddle, David.
        Tenorman : a novella / by David Huddle.
              p.   cm.
        ISBN 0-8118-1027-5
        I. Title.
PS3558.U287T46   1995
813'.54—dc20   95-12601
                                                      CIP

Book design and composition: Gretchen Scoble
Jacket Illustration: Jeffrey Fisher

Distributed in Canada by Raincoast Books
8680 Cambie Street
Vancouver, BC V6P 6M9

10 9 8 7 6 5 4 3 2 1

Chronicle Books
275 Fifth Street
San Francisco, CA 94103

For Molly

I

When Carnes got out of the hospital in Stockholm, we offered him the horn of his choice, the studio of his dreams, and luxurious support for as long as he stayed clean. At the time, Carnes was 59 years old, but he looked closer to seventy. During the worst winter of his life, a couple of days before somebody checked him into the hospital, he had hocked his old horn. When we talked to him, he still vividly remembered having almost died on the streets of Göteborg. He was ready to consider what we had to offer him.

The first condition of our agreement was that he had to move back to the States—we wanted him in the Washington area, within driving distance of the museum's main office. He wasn't eager to come back to "Ol' Virginny," as he put it, but our deal must have seemed like his own customized version of paradise: a comfortable place to live; whatever he wanted in the way of food, clothes, books, records, and so on; along with an ideal working circumstance and all the time he wanted to spend with this replacement tenor he had asked for.

He already had that horn on his wish list, a Selmer Mark VI, vintage 1957, that Getz had played for a couple of years and that some private collector in Stockholm had picked up and let Carnes try out one afternoon some years back. How much of the American taxpayers' money we had to pay for that saxophone is still a confidential matter.

Carnes wondered if he could live in his studio. "I want to hole up for a while, gentlemen. I just want to stay put." We couldn't have asked for a better inclination on his part.

So we found a large duplex in Chevy Chase and had half of it fixed up just as he described it, a small kitchen with a big window that looked out onto a backyard garden, a neat little living area with a waterbed for his bad back, and a first-rate stereo—he didn't necessarily want big speakers or a powerful amplifier, but he did ask for "the best sound you gentlemen can get for me." And he did accept a CD player after we told him it would be easier to obtain the recordings he wanted on CD rather than on vinyl. But no TV, no wet bar, and not much in the way of art. We gave him the tour late one afternoon when the light was angling in through the windows. "Feels fine, gentlemen," he said, walking around and touching things, plunking a few keys on the piano.

There was no shortage of young musicians who wanted a chance to spend time around Carnes, to study with him, as it were. We turned away lots of them who'd just heard about our project, people whose names you probably would know if you listen seriously to jazz. Carnes was this living landmark of the music, an artist already of forty years' consequence, who had reached the apex of his genius here at the end of his life. We had our pick of the New York prodigies, the kids who'd been brought along by Wynton Marsalis and his dad. Our grant provided money to pay musicians top wages just to be available to Carnes when he wished for their assistance in his composing, his arranging, his noodling around in his art.

So when Carnes said, "Send me in that piano man," Cody Jones, our gifted twenty-two-year-old pianist, presented himself at the studio door. Then Carnes and Cody could work on a piece as long as the old man wanted to. If Carnes decided they needed a bassist, they summoned Wil Stanfield, who appeared with his instrument, pleased to have been called and eager to jam with Carnes. Ditto with Curtis Wells, our Juilliard dropout drummer. And so on. Wynton himself came down from New York occasionally and sent word in to the old man that he was available; Carnes appreciated that and always asked him to step right in.

He liked Wynton, respected what he'd done for jazz. The two of them spent as much time talking as they did playing music.

When he had tired them out—he himself was apparently indefatigable—Carnes thanked the young musicians, laconically advised them to stay away from drugs, drink, and loose women; raised a gnarled old hand; and told them "later." Then he played to himself and to the empty studio for another hour, or two hours, or all night if he wanted. Some nights—or early mornings—he set down his compositions or made notes for them, a kind of scoring only he seemed to understand. But usually he relied on his memory and set down nothing. He did exactly what he wanted to, and whatever it was, it suited us. We videotaped and recorded everything he did, every sound he made. Except for when he went to the bathroom. We could have done that, too, if we'd wanted; Carnes didn't care about the recording and videotaping part of the project; he seemed happy doing what he was doing, living inside his music.

We didn't talk about it much among ourselves, but I know that most of us on the team were pretty proud of what we'd done, rescuing this wonderful old guy, bringing him home to the U.S.A., nourishing his work and preserving it for posterity. If it hadn't been for us and our project, Carnes most likely would have been sleeping on a steam vent in Göteborg. Or been frozen to death and locked up in some morgue drawer in Stockholm, waiting for next-of-kin to send for the body.

A significant part of our project was that Sony-CBS provided us with state-of-the-art equipment. They let us use this amazing machinery; the stuff in our studio half of the duplex was huge—we'd had to knock down a couple of walls to make room for it—but our cameras took up so little room in Carnes's apartment and were so unobtrusive that he seldom took note of them.

Our musicologists and recording specialists worked on editing and assembling the work of the old tenorman—including random observations he made in conversations with the younger musicians and with Wynton—into archives and professional recordings. The income from these recordings would go into his estate; there would be more than enough to provide comfortably for generations of the old man's heirs, if he had any.

Carnes didn't like talking too much business with us. He said he just wanted to work. And we made it so that he didn't have to bother himself with any of the petty matters of preserving and marketing his work. He simply did what he pleased and asked for whatever he wanted—which, given the infinite possibilities available to him, wasn't really very much. What he asked for we brought to him, almost instantly.

For a while our only difficulty was that the old man had developed a taste for fresh fruit and sometimes wanted it at odd hours. Finally, we worked out a deal with one of the grocery suppliers in the D.C. area. Every morning they sent over their truck and let us select the best of their fruit, which came from all over the world.

Carnes told our musical historian that, from about the age of ten on, this was the cleanest year of his life. Coffee was his only vice. At night, an hour or two before he went to bed, he drank tea while he listened to his stereo. In those late hours, he favored the recordings of Ben Webster and Coleman Hawkins. "My old pals," he called them. "Gents," he'd say, "I'm gonna spend a little time with the Hawk now," and of course we'd clear out for him.

He liked listening to his records by himself. And of course what he played was of interest to our people, too. We kept track of his choices and matched them against the compositions he was producing during those months. A couple of our more scholarly team members were fascinated with that aspect of his *creative process*, a term, incidentally, that never failed to bring a droll expression onto Carnes's face whenever somebody used it around him. "My process," he'd repeat after one of our guys and draw his mouth down and kind of grin.

Why we didn't anticipate that the old guy might wish the company of a woman none of us knew. In retrospect, it astonishes us that we didn't, though our having no women on our team probably had a lot to do with it. Most of us had wives or girlfriends or partners, but for some reason we figured a working genius didn't need a significant other.

Historically, Carnes had never had anything to do with women musicians—not that there had been that many female instrumentalists in jazz in his day. Years before, he had been quoted as saying he didn't like to work with singers, male or female, because just about the time he knew where he was going with his solo, the singer would be ready to pick up the vocal again. But of course he'd had a couple of wives and plenty of girlfriends. So we should have anticipated how he'd be—opposite sex-wise—when he came clean.

About this matter of a woman, we were stupid—there wasn't one of us who wouldn't admit it.

Months had passed. We were all fond of Carnes. He was a dear guy, and he seemed to like most of our team members. Something that impressed him was that everybody on the project knew his music—we could remind him of a tune he'd recorded with Ray Brown and Tommy Flanagan in 1959, when he might not remember anything more than the way the notes came to him through his embouchure and his fingers when he picked up his horn.

Something else that seemed to please him secretly was how much all of us on the Project respected him. He'd had years of getting used to dealing with people who knew him as just a guy in a band and wouldn't have dreamed he was a major American artist. Now with us, he had to beg us to stop calling him "sir" and "Mr. Carnes." "'Ed,'" he'd say, "I want you to call me 'Ed.' And don't say 'sir' to me. I *work* for a living." But it was evident that he appreciated the way we honored him with our manners. We weren't putting on an act for him; we were on the Project because we loved the music of Edgar DeWeese Carnes.

"Gentlemen, you've been awfully good to me. I don't deny that for a minute. I'm not complaining here. And I don't want you to think I'm pulling out a surprise. This isn't anything I thought of when we first talked about our arrangement. It's something that came to me this past week—because I'm getting somewhere in my music. I had to play for my living, so I couldn't ever sit back and think about it, make one thing build onto the next. So if this is a surprise, it's a surprise to me, too. But what it comes down to is that I need something very similar to a girlfriend.

"I don't mean I want you to go out and get me some woman off the street. And I don't mean I want you to find me some pretty widow out of the church choir. I just need the company of an *interesting* woman. You know what I mean? Hard for me to explain to you what that is, if you don't know already. But somebody I can talk to. Not necessarily about music. But she'd have to know something about that, too. Don't want some tone-deaf Marylou in here trying to tell me about current events. I swear I don't know how to tell you. I'd go out and find her myself, except I know I'd find some other things while I was at it. Won't do for me to be going to the

8

clubs looking for company. You gentlemen have to go out and find her for me, and I don't even know how to tell you what she looks like."

Who could blame Carnes for what he wanted? We understood his request perfectly well, but we weren't sure how to go about granting it. No one on our staff could quite imagine himself going out to the jazz clubs in search of female companionship for our man.

Cody Jones threw back his head and laughed out loud when someone asked him what he thought. "I think it's time for a party is what I think," Cody said.

"Good idea," our director said when he heard Cody's suggestion. "Henry," he said to me, "I think you need to make the arrangements for a party where Mr. Carnes might meet someone who interests him."

I knew, of course, that if this party were a success, my director would receive full credit for it and that if it flopped, I would be held responsible. I had no quarrel with that. From my first day of working with this director, I had understood the nature of being his assistant. Nevertheless, the racial complication made the assignment difficult: a thirty-five-year-old white guy throwing a party where a sixty-year-old black guy would enjoy himself.

As a child growing up in Welch, West Virginia, I took piano lessons until my teacher confided to my father that he was wasting his money on my musical future. I hold a B.A. in government studies from the University of Virginia and an M.A. in Fine Arts Management from American University. My wife and I live in a raised ranch in Fairfax, Virginia, in a neighborhood that is 95 percent white. No more than three or four black people have attended any social gathering to which I have been invited.

My relationship with jazz has been informed by my paranoiac intuition that blacks despise whites, coupled with my yearning to know how blacks suffer their lives with such grace. I've had very few black friends. The night after my boss informed me that I was to be responsible for it, I dreamed about this party—a sort of sixties vision of blacks and whites and Asians and Native Americans all talking intensely and eating and laughing and dancing and enjoying each other's company, the whole undulating panorama shimmering in extravagant colors. The background music was Carnes's "Scandinavian Suite." Carnes himself—elegantly dressed, ebullient, garrulous, and utterly charming—was at the center of the gathering, surrounded by women of various ethnic backgrounds. Acting as his translator, with Carnes's arm draped across my shoulder, I communicated his witty and inscrutable observations to these women. My dream did not provide me with an explanation for why Carnes needed a translator.

I cannot imitate his speech patterns. He grew up in Buffalo, New York, and since he'd dropped out of high school, his language wasn't quite up to the level of his intellectual development; nevertheless, in his own way he was quite an articulate man.

"A party, huh?" Carnes said when I went in at breakfast to tell him that we were thinking of having a gathering in his honor and that we would like to have his thoughts about what kind of party it should be. "You thinking about having it here or somewhere else? You don't know? Well, Henry, I'll tell you, around here is pretty familiar to me.

"Some years ago I went to this reception for Mr. Ellington at an embassy in Brussels, Belgium. That place scared me so bad I had to drink every little glass of champagne I could lift off those little trays they were passing by us. I disgraced myself before I ever got to say hello to that man who had meant everything that mattered to me. I had so much to ask Mr. Ellington, questions I'd been saving up to ask him. My one chance to talk with him, and there I was so drunk that when I stumbled up to speak, he turned away from me, turned his back on me. I won't ever forget that.

"But aside from me being a drunk anyway, I blame it on all those pictures on the wall, those cold floors, bright lights, and nowhere to sit down.

"If you can get one of these boys here who's got his own place in town, somebody who wouldn't mind having a party at his house, why that might be nice. I'd like there to be a sofa where

I can sit down and not have to be spitting in people's faces when I talk to them. If the talk gets just right, why then I don't miss Mr. Booze so much.

"You know I come from a family of quick-tempered people on both sides. My mother and my father, especially when they were young, it didn't take anything to get them riled up. They'd start saying things they'd know they were going to regret. To their own children they'd say what you wouldn't whisper to a yard dog barking at you from under somebody's front porch. They knew better; they just did it anyway.

"So I was like that, too, I learned from them—I had it in me anyway. When I was a young man, my temper was a crazy thing ready to fly out of my head any minute.

"I did temper things, too, used to try to hit people, even though I was the world's worst fighter. Then I'd have a drink to calm myself down. What I told myself was, I'll have this drink, then I won't be so mad anymore. That much of it was right; I'd forget about what I was mad about and who I was mad at. But then I'd get mad at somebody else over something they said, and I'd be drunk by then and not making any sense.

"Good thing my mother and father let me learn how to play a horn. I wasn't cut out to be a boxer, I'll tell you that much. I hit this bass player one time, a kid named Herman Drexler from Rochester, hit him right in the mouth with my fist. Herman Drexler wiped off his mouth and looked at his hand to see if he was bleeding. He saw he was, then he popped me one right in the forehead. It knocked me back about ten feet before I went down to the floor. I'd never been hit like that. Herman walked up and looked down at me and said, 'I would have hit you in the mouth except you wouldn't be able to play.' I said, 'Thank you, Herman, I appreciate that.' And I did. He and I played that night in the same band again, both of us paying special attention to what we were telling each other in the music. And we didn't play bad, either. But I never did hit anybody again after that. Herman taught me. It's easy to learn not to hit anybody compared to what it takes to learn not to drink anymore. I still want a drink every day. I just don't want one worse than I do want one. Sometimes it's close between want and don't want.

"Only thing I've still got with me that I want to hold on to now is playing this horn. Everything else, it's okay with me for it to be gone. Especially drinking. I hope it stays gone."

Carnes is a relatively small man, five foot ten or so, with a substantial belly. He keeps his hair short, and he doesn't have much of it anyway. Most of his scalp has a polished look to it. His skin is various shades of reddish brown, like stained oak, his face somewhere between medium and light brown and his hands very light skinned. His hands are surprisingly small.

"Hands like these," he says, holding them up for exhibition, "I should be playing alto." He puts his hands on his knees. "But I don't like the upper register, don't like the sound of it. On tenor, I have to sacrifice some of the low notes, that low B-flat, unless I just have to have it. My hands are strong, but these fingers don't stretch the way a tenorman's ought to." He wiggles the little finger of his left hand and laughs when Bob Fulton, one of our technical people, leans forward to get a close look at that treasure of a pinky of his.

"Got my mother's hands." Carnes shakes his head. "What'd I get from my father? No, he wasn't any kind of a musician—everybody guesses that he must have been. But here's how he was. Anywhere we went where somebody was playing an instrument or singing, my father would stop and listen. He would be quiet, and he wouldn't pay any attention to us when we tried to hurry him along. Two old white women playing violin duets in a shopping mall, my father would find a bench, sit there, and listen half the afternoon. Salvation Army band playing in their overcoats on a corner, my father would stand in the snow, listening, listening. College boy strumming a banjo on his landlady's porch, kitchen help practicing their harmony while they take a break in the alley, church choir running through Sunday's hymns on a Thursday night, it didn't matter, my father stopped and listened. Sometimes we'd just have to leave him sitting or standing where he was and come back later.

"Thing about it is, I don't really know what my father was hearing. He didn't tap his foot, he didn't nod his head, he didn't smile or frown, he didn't even applaud when the song was finished and everybody else was clapping their hands. He'd sit and wait for what else was going to be played. My father had this infinite patience. But he almost never talked about the music, never explained why he listened to it like that.

"Except this one time, after we'd come home from downtown Buffalo. I was pestering him about why he'd stood around listening to this hammering dulcimer player outside a music store. I was about twelve years old then; I'd been playing in my school band for about a year. I thought I was hot stuff on that old banged-up school-band saxophone. 'Daddy,' I said, 'why you even listening to that old hillbilly music, la-te-da-te-da?'

"He looked over his glasses at me—he was a schoolteacher and had a way of looking at you when he wanted to. 'It's what a human being has inside,' he said. 'I know I don't know as much about music as you do, but I also know that when I hear somebody playing—not on the radio or on a record but right there themselves—I have to listen to it. I know I need to do that.'

"My father was quiet a while, looking at me. I didn't have anything to say back to him, either, because I was so surprised he'd explained anything to me about it. I hadn't expected him to answer me on that topic because he never had before when I'd pestered him. 'I couldn't say that there's much in this world that I know for sure, but I do know that.' His voice was real low like he might have been telling me something, or maybe he just needed to say something out loud. 'I know I need to listen when somebody plays. And I never heard any kind of music that somebody played that I didn't think, All right, a man may be a bad thing, but at least he has that inside him.'

"When I think back about him now, I don't ever remember him humming or whistling or singing in church or any of those things. My father was a nonmusical man, if you can feature such a creature—ha! But music meant more to him than it does to most people." Carnes shook his head. "I guess I didn't have much choice but to pick up a horn and stick with it," he said. And even as he was talking, I was aware of how his words were being recorded. I could envision the text, the black alphabet spinning out into the future on the white page of a book that would be published not so many years from when we were just sitting there talking at his little kitchen table.

That was the first time our project ever seemed to me like some very subtle thievery or embezzlement we were practicing, with Carnes the victim.

II

"I don't think that's the case at all," Marianne told me. The evening after my conversation with Carnes about his father, she and I were talking over coffee and dessert at Bottelli's, where we had met for dinner.

"You saved this man, not merely from obscurity but also from an ignominious death. He's better off than he ever has been, the people who appreciate his music are delighted to have him still playing, and you're doing work you love. Tell me who's being hurt by this project. Even the taxpayers ought to be happy to have their dollars supporting an artist instead of a general or a politician." She doesn't add "a bureaucrat," and I appreciate that.

My wife teaches law at Georgetown. In a woman a shade over six feet tall, whose eyes are that blazing blue of a romantic, a fanatic, a seer, Marianne's common sense is disconcerting. Thin, pale, and discriminating in her wardrobe but eschewing makeup or any attention to her dark hair beyond washing and brushing it, she is not someone you expect to speak to you like the proverbial old farmer leaning on the barnyard fence.

The first time I saw her—on the other side of a D.C. apartment dining room at a party—I fantasized a woman who'd walk up to me and say, "Do you have plans for this weekend? And by the way, what is your name?" Three minutes later I glanced at her again and imagined the same woman walking up to ask if I had yet taken Jesus for my personal savior.

Her appearance suggests the irrational—I suspect that it's her height even more than her eyes. You expect her to be reckless, flagrantly disregardful of convention, some variety of a missionary or ideological extremist. You remark that woman as the dangerous one, the one you'd follow against your better judgment.

What Marianne did say that evening, when I finally located someone who would introduce us, was, "I have to go home now. Paper due tomorrow in Intellectual Properties." (She was a student in those days.) "Very pleased to make your acquaintance." Then she shook hands with me, hello and good-bye all at the same time, with a hand neither warm nor cold, but very slender, very pale. Brief and formal as my initial encounter with Marianne Stettler was, she nevertheless gave me the flicker of a conspiratorial look. The next day and the day after that, I was hearing her voice and remembering her lifted eyebrows, her high forehead.

Three days after the party, I went to a lot of trouble to get her phone number and called her up. We don't—either of us—understand what she saw in me that made her agree to go out with me. Whatever personal trait it was must also have been the same quality that eventually persuaded her to marry me. We guess it was my conversational ability, or rather the fact that I listened to her when her peers seemed to be listening to the person they thought she was.

I still have the power to hear Marianne with a more exact understanding than most of her acquaintances, so that when she needs to be heard, she counts on my doing that for her.

Other aspects of our relationship are—to our sorrow—less dependable. After the first months of our marriage, the two of us discovered ourselves to be sexually fastidious. Rarely now do we find ourselves in the mood at the same time, though we each have mournfully admitted to the other that we'd be better off if we had more sex. It's just that neither of us can stand merely to accommodate the other—or to be merely accommodated by the other. We'd probably have divorced years ago except for our mutually confessed suspicion that other lovers would find our finicky ways much less tolerable than we do. Thus our incompatibility has become a cruel form of compatibility.

In the natural pause of our waiter's warming our cups with fresh coffee, I decided to shift the topic of conversation to what was really on my mind. "Mr. Carnes has requested female company," I told Marianne. Then I watched her face to see what it would tell me before she delivered a spoken response. There came the thinnest of smiles—a teasing acknowledgment that any idiots should have anticipated that sooner or later Carnes would have wanted female company.

"I—want—a—woman!" Marianne gleefully whisper-shouted. She was referring to that Fellini movie where the boy-hero's uncle climbs a tree and shouts, again and again, forlornly, out into the desolate landscape. "I want a woman!" is a landmark reference for Marianne and me, a dramatic metaphor for something we understand to account for what happens in the world that we find of interest. She and I were intensely interested in all sorts of sexual behavior; we passed through a phase of regularly watching nature programs on TV, just to inform ourselves of the mating procedures of animals, birds, insects, reptiles, and so on. We found it somewhat reassuring that there was nothing about watching monkeys or arctic foxes do it that made us want to do it.

As a result of our informal research, Marianne and I have convinced ourselves that almost every human couple we know has its difficulties; almost every individual of our acquaintance seems to us, when we really think about it, painfully isolated. As dreadful as our own circumstance is, we count ourselves better off than most.

Marianne's tone shifted to sarcasm. "Haven't you guys ever listened to his music?"

Of course I asked her what she meant.

"What do I mean?" Marianne drummed her slender fingers on the tablecloth, smiling toward the ceiling, as if addressing a guardian angel who certainly wouldn't have had to ask her what she meant. "Maybe you can't hear it because you're guys! Maybe that's why I can hear it, even though it's not my kind of music, and I've never met the man."

Here Marianne turned a droll face toward me because she felt that I should have made some occasion for her personally to meet the man whose music has commanded the last several years of my professional energies. It isn't that I don't want her to meet Carnes; it is merely the case that all of us involved in the project have taken pains not to parade him in front of our friends and relatives.

It occurred to me that in our considering Carnes such a prize, perhaps we have denied him the acquaintance of people he might very well enjoy meeting—like Marianne. I knew that most of my colleagues' wives and girlfriends thought of him exactly as Marianne did, as a quaint, little old black man whom they'd like to shake hands with just to satisfy some mild curiosity. My colleagues and I had confided to each other that our wives and girlfriends didn't love the music. Thus our informal agreement not to bring them in to meet him. And we didn't expect them to love the music. Either you loved it or you didn't, we told each other.

Sitting comfortably with my wife in Bottelli's, it also occurred to me that it is men who love what Carnes plays, men who are devoted to him.

"Let me just say," Marianne said, "that that time you played all those Carnes tapes for me, I had this fleeting notion that if music could unhook a bra, a good many of Mr. Carnes's female listeners would experience a sudden loosening of their undergarments."

When I asked why she hadn't told me what she thought at the time I'd played the tapes for her, she merely smiled and shrugged.

"So does that account for why you were less than enthusiastic about his music?" I asked her.

The little wrinkle that appeared between Marianne's eyebrows told me that she was taking the question seriously. "Maybe it does," she said, toying with her coffee spoon. "I didn't think it through at the time, but here's how it must be. As a woman, you sense that you're the *object* of that music. The crudest example I can think of would be if you walk by a construction site in the city and suddenly you're the object of the whistling and hooting

22

and leering of a bunch of workers sitting around with their lunch pails and their cigarettes. You have a choice of walking on or confronting the bastards or stopping to try to embarrass them with a friendly chat. The least complicated response is to keep walking.

"So that's how, if you're a woman, you might decide to respond to Carnes's music, even though it's very polite, very elegant, very seductive. It's not construction workers in hard hats; it's male models in tuxedos, leaning over and whispering softly into your ear, asking if they can fetch you any little thing. But the issue is exactly the same. A woman might decide, as I instinctively decided, to take note of that music but just not to get involved. Because that's the least complicated way for a woman to deal with what she's hearing. But there must also be the woman who says to herself, 'Hey, this stuff is gorgeous, and it's all for me. I have to listen to this man play. I don't have any choice.'"

"So a man and a woman listening to Carnes play would hear two different tunes, even though they'd be listening to the same sounds at the same time?"

Marianne shrugged and sipped the last of her coffee. "It's not a point I'd want to argue in court," she said. "It's just what I think right now. How are you guys going to find him some female company?" she asked. "Got any pimps on the staff?"

Talking with Marianne can, at any moment, turn into an adventure. In spite of our years of marriage, in spite of our understanding of each other in certain areas of thought and feeling, I find that I can't depend on my estimates of our conversational relationship. I may think that she and I are in perfect accord—as we usually are—when beneath our literal words we are actually carrying on an old argument. I may think that I am setting forth a proposition that she will certainly, vehemently reject, only to discover that in fact I am expressing thoughts she has been keeping to herself for months. "Wait a minute," I will plead. "Are we arguing or agreeing?"

"Both. Neither. Whatever," she will say and kiss me on one cheek while pretending to slap me on the other. In such moments, though they are metaphysically disconcerting and though I never tell her so, Marianne is utterly charming.

"We are going to give a party in Mr. Carnes's honor," I told her. "You are finally going to meet the man himself."

"I'll wear two bras," she said. "Or else no bra at all." I could tell that the idea of a party for Carnes had exhilarated Marianne.

I saw that we had achieved one of those remarkable episodes of mood synchronization, but I had to remind myself that it wouldn't last until we got home—or even, for that matter, until we reached the lot behind Bottelli's, where our separate cars were parked.

III

CODY JONES HAD DRIVEN the old man up to Baltimore to shop. For Carnes, they'd purchased a deep maroon suede blazer, a matching tie designed to look like a work of art, a custom-fitted pair of black flannel pants, a white tab-collar shirt, and a pair of cordovan-and-white wing-tip shoes. Thus the unkempt genius of our project studio had been transmogrified into the trim and brilliant young man-of-the-world of his 1963 publicity photos. Freshly barbered and shaved, he walked into that party with a swagger and glide I'd never seen before.

"Here he is," Marianne whispered—we were standing arm in arm—and this was the first time she'd ever seen him. She might not have consciously decided to do so, but she began moving us in his direction.

Others in the room were apparently similarly affected by our resplendent guest of honor. When we came up to him, we were joining a cluster of well-wishers. Carnes stood at the center, shaking hands with strangers and embracing old friends. "Very pleased, very pleased," he was saying, ". . . nice of the Stanfields to open their home to this old expatriate reprobate."

Because Marianne is so tall—a couple of inches taller than me—people in crowds generally make way for her. When Carnes turned our way, he exaggerated how far he had to lean back to look up into her face. She'd chosen a short black velvet sheath of a dress that accentuated her greyhound thinness. She wore no makeup, but she'd brushed her hair into uncommon shininess and she'd worn her white-gold earrings with the matching neck-lace that seemed to be pulling the room's light toward her pale face and slender neck.

"Well now," rumbled Carnes, his ordinary voice deepened to a rich baritone. "I believe I am just about to meet the Countess of Verticality. You must be Henry's wife; I see him clutching onto your elbow like he has to keep you from float-ing away from us. Eddie Carnes, your highness. Very pleased to meet you."

"Do you really think of yourself as an expatriate, Mr. Carnes?" Marianne asked as she withdrew her hand from his.

Carnes's eyebrows lifted; he put his hands in his pockets and leaned back on his heels, looking slowly from one to the other of the men and women clustered around him.

Wil Stanfield approached the group, accompanied by a woman who caught and held Carnes's attention. She had lightly freckled skin the color of a ginger cookie, and she wore a strand of pearls with a yellow silk blouse. Her straightened hair had been dyed a dark red and extravagantly swirled up and around her head. When she came up to us, Carnes addressed her. "What do you think, young lady? Am I an expatriate?"

The look this not-especially-young woman gave Carnes was something like a smile—Marianne later explained to me that it was a smile with *background,* an expression that told Carnes she had lived through too much for smiling to be a simple matter but that, in deference to him and out of general politeness, she would try to participate in the occasion he had just constructed. Her face also seemed to instruct him that he could get by with only so much of this kind of behavior with her. She spoke in a low voice. "Well, Mr. Carnes, when was the last time you felt at home?"

He snorted, as if half-amused and half-insulted by her counter question. "Last time I felt at home," he mused and shook his head. The look he then gave the woman became steady, though I can't say what I thought Carnes meant to convey to her, perhaps that he recognized her good sense and that he was certain the two of them understood each other.

"You're Wil Stanfield's cousin, aren't you?" he said, reaching for her hand.

She nodded. Not conventionally pretty, she was a woman Marianne and I probably would have remarked even if she hadn't been noticed by Carnes. Her silk blouse and straight skirt set off her figure. There was a proud way she held her head that made me understand why she went to such trouble to have her hair styled up off her neck.

"Thelma Watkins."

She nodded again, or rather bowed her head toward Carnes. "You know my name?"

Carnes nodded at Wil Stanfield, flashed a smile, and held onto Thelma Watkins's hand. "He mentioned you a couple of times. Said he thinks a lot of you, said you helped him through the difficulties of his former life." Again, Carnes snorted, meaning, I supposed, that such difficulties were familiar to him. Then he blinked and widened his eyes. "Sometimes I pay attention to what my good men tell me. Selective attention, I guess you'd call it. Can I freshen your drink, Ms. Watkins? I already see that I'm going to have to invent my own ginger ale because none of these thoughtful boys can seem to discover it for me."

The two of them walked away from us, toward the Stanfields' kitchen. "Why don't one of you boys put on a record for this party?" Carnes waved at Curtis Wells and Cody Jones, who were taking an inventory of Wil Stanfield's CD collection.

"Does he have that Art Tatum/Ben Webster you all played for me the other day? I'd like for Mr. Tatum and Mr. Webster to help me talk to this young lady." Though his voice was pitched low, it carried across the room.

With her head slightly bowed, Thelma Watkins walked beside him. I couldn't tell if that was from her embarrassment at Carnes's display of interest or from smiling to herself and wishing to hide it. Though his fingers must have been touching the back of her arm, she and Carnes kept a decorous distance from each other. But there already seemed to be a strand of intimacy between them.

"Quick work," sighed Marianne. I knew she wished she had held more of Carnes's attention—I knew she had expected to hold more of his attention. But then she brightened and turned to me. "But I helped, didn't I? I was the one who asked the question that got them going!" The tension that had informed her posture and voice had been replaced with a loosey-goosey exuberance. I left her in the company of Curtis Wells and his girlfriend while I went to refill our drinks.

Later, when we talked it over, Marianne and I agreed that Carnes's meeting with Thelma Watkins at the party had what we called *dramatic content*. Anyone carefully observing it would have remarked it as an event of significance. Soon afterward, the rooms of the house filled to capacity; in the resulting body-to-body intimacy, the party took on such a generous spirit that it actually resembled my absurd dream of a multicultural paradise.

I'd had the good luck to accept Curtis Wells's suggestion to hire his girlfriend's father as our caterer. This Mr. Willaford was a genius of barbecuing pork, seasoning potato salad, and serving country cooking as a stylish cocktail buffet. Early in the evening the mayor of Washington dropped by to meet and to chat with Carnes, but to all the musicians' relief, she had to hurry away to another social engagement.

All this while, circulating through the rooms, speaking with one guest and another, Carnes showed himself to be aware of Thelma Watkins, to be "in touch" with her, as if they carried tiny wireless communication devices. In Carnes it wasn't difficult to see the signs of this connection; he seemed to want it to be visible. However, Ms. Watkins was subtle to the point of inscrutability. Marianne claims to have observed plenty of evidence of Ms. Watkins' interest in our guest of honor—Ms. Watkins was usually in the same room as Carnes and she usually was at least partially turned toward him. But I noticed nothing special in her behavior. Of course everyone was drawn toward Carnes, everyone seemed to be keeping an eye on him.

The surprise of the evening was the appearance of Wynton and his brother Branford—apparently willing to give up their commitment for the sake of this evening's celebration—who were dramatically presented by Wil Stanfield when he opened the set of double doors to his music studio (they had been closed until this moment). The distinguished siblings held their instruments ready and immediately launched a duet of Carnes's signature tune, "Buffalo Stampede." They riffed through it once with astonishing alacrity, then finished so abruptly that for a shocked moment the whole house rang with silence. Carnes himself broke it by cracking his hands together in loud applause.

Whether or not Carnes knew that the Marsalis brothers were going to appear as they did, he acted as if he had rehearsed the whole thing with them. He and Cody Jones stepped into the studio. Carnes's horn was already assembled and ready for him on a stand. Cody took the piano bench; Curtis Wells mounted the waiting set of drums; Wil Stanfield took up his bass; and after some tuning and murmuring with each other, the little band broke into another familiar Carnes tune, "Midnight Sunrise."

Live jazz so intoxicates me that I become happy, childish, and downright stupefied. The energy of the music that the Marsalis/Carnes combo played that evening plugged directly into some socket of my sensibility. Carnes and Wynton and Branford traded more and more intricate eight-bar solos, then the three of them riffed in varying patterns of harmony, unison, and counterpoint, as if they'd practiced these numbers for months when the fact was they were probably playing them—inventing them!—together for the first time ever.

Marianne is the only person to whom I've ever tried to explain my feelings about live jazz. The metaphor I chose was a field I played in as a child, a field that had the power to make me feel happy. Actually, this was a hillside meadow, sowed in alfalfa and occasionally cut and bailed. In the middle of it was an area where I could stand and look out over our little town of Welch, West Virginia, about half a mile away. For the one who stood right there, the landscape held ten thousand extremely vivid details; it could be considered for hours, and some of it could be held in mind for many days at a time, but since it could never be completely absorbed, it was permanently fresh and interesting. The field held me and me alone in its enormous palm. When I had studied the vista until my head was filled with it, I lay down in the alfalfa and gave myself over to the breeze and the sunlight. A freedom came into me. I felt my life to be rich with possibility, that whatever I wished would drift my way as surely as the clouds sailed across the sky.

A similar exhilaration came over me as I listened to Carnes and his supporting musicians. Though I lost my awareness of the party, Marianne stayed alert to what was happening. She told me later that about halfway through the third number, just as Carnes was about to finish his solo in "Cat's Cradle," Thelma Watkins slid away from her place in the audience and walked back through a swinging door into the kitchen. Unless she meant to signal to Carnes that she had no use for his music, I couldn't imagine why she would have done such a thing. Marianne, though, had considered Ms. Watkins's behavior and thought she understood it.

"It's just what I was telling you, Henry. I'm sure your genius's music doesn't have the same effect on men, but a woman has to choose whether she's going to submit to it or not. And I can imagine what it would be like if Carnes had focused in on me the way he did that woman. When I saw her leave the room, it broke a spell that was starting to work on me. I'd been standing there beside you—and I knew you'd 'lifted off' the way you do when one of your old jazz guys picks up a horn and starts to play. You were up there in the zone, and I was thinking that now I understood the power that music has over you. I had started entertaining this fantasy of walking right up front, right up in front of Carnes, and just standing there with my arms wide open—like, Did you call, sir? Well, here I am. I'd been thinking, What would he do if I walked up there like that? I was thinking of it as a kind of joke.

"But I understand this now: It wasn't just some silly little joke that occurred to me and wasn't some random fantasy that just appeared in my brain out of nowhere. In this case, I'll bet that almost every woman there was feeling the same impulse. It's physiological! I'll bet if you had the right kind of equipment, you could track it scientifically, the places in his music where Carnes sends out his message: *Come to me, all you ladies.*"

"So in your view, Marianne, Thelma Watkins chose to retreat to the kitchen when the signal Carnes was sending her was a directive to come to the front of the crowd? Should we interpret her retreat as a signal to him that she isn't interested in him?"

"You're a man. I shouldn't have expected you to understand."

"All you have to do is explain it to me."

"No self-respecting woman wants to respond to a general effort at seduction. Sure, girls threw their underpants at Elvis, but somewhere around the age seventeen, you begin to understand that it isn't in your best interests to behave like that. You want the man who wants you to be wanting only you, not a whole roomful of females. You learn to discern just how individualized a man's desire for you is."

"So Thelma Watkins found Carnes's mating signal a bit too generic for her taste."

"That's a crude way to put it."

"But that's what you mean, isn't it?"

"Approximately."

In my circulating through the party on my own, I managed to find an opportunity to quiz Wil Stanfield about Ms. Watkins. When he talked about his cousin, it was evident that he looked up to her, that in his eyes she was a heroine.

For the past twenty years, Thelma Stanfield Watkins had been an English teacher at Mount Vernon High School in Washington. She was as much a legend locally as Carnes was in the world of jazz. She taught the college preparatory sections of senior English. If a young black man or woman at Mount Vernon had hopes of gaining admission to a college, he or she was placed in one of Ms. Watkins's classes, and he or she had to make the grade under Ms. Watkins. The grade was a B; when she gave a student at least a B (and not a B-), she designated the student as a candidate for college.

All up and down the east coast, college-admissions officers had come to understand and to respect Thelma Watkins's standard of grading. College football and basketball coaches knew about her to the extent that when they talked with an athlete from Mount Vernon—a high school with a longstanding reputation of graduating fine athletes—they knew to ask what grade in English the recruit expected or hoped to receive from Ms. Watkins.

Some weeks later I learned from Wil Stanfield that Thelma had been married for twelve years to Nelson Watkins, a white man, a journalist, who had gradually come to treat her badly because of her refusal to have his children. Watkins's bad treatment of Thelma had been mostly in the form of psychological abuse. Thelma's refusal to have his children had originally been intuitive, but over the course of some years had become a matter of conviction: Watkins wanted to father children with black blood so as to outrage his old-South family—and particularly his father who was the mayor of Six Mile, South Carolina. Wil told me that Thelma had wanted children, and at first had even wanted Watkins's children, but not on those terms.

Thelma's truncated marriage to Watkins had left her childless and more than usually skeptical of men. The experience hadn't improved her view of the white race either, Stanfield told me, though he supposed that because she was a teacher, she was accustomed to battling prejudice, within herself as well as in the world around her. "She's not bitter," he explained to me, "but if she didn't fight it so hard, she would be."

These things and more Marianne and I later came to know about Thelma Watkins. At the party at Wil Stanfield's home, we witnessed a kind of romantic maneuvering between her and Carnes that we recognized as elegant, even poignant, in its restraint, its wariness, its being so deeply informed by the complex personal histories of both would-be lovers.

A couple of days after the party, I had occasion to ask Carnes if he had taken note of Ms. Watkins's leaving the room during his solo in "Cat's Cradle."

He chuckled. "When I saw her step back into that kitchen, I knew she and I had us a little something. I had thought maybe we did—I hoped we did—but until then, I didn't know it for sure."

IV

My notes indicate that a week after the party in Carnes's honor, Whitney Ballston, our historical consultant, made the following observation in an informal discussion at the Project's main office: "It's like somebody else, like another human being entirely. There are no precedents anywhere in all of Mr. Carnes's recordings for this 'enlarged' sound or these bizarre composition patterns, or even for the energy in his playing right now. There's even a new way he's using silence, letting half or three quarters of a phrase stand and then picking it up out of nowhere as if he'd been playing a whole sequence of notes in his mind without putting them through the horn. Yesterday I asked him if he'd changed mouthpieces or the weight of his reed or anything like that, and he just laughed at me."

Phil Hughes, our chief recording engineer, then spoke as follows: "I'm wondering if maybe we ought not to call in a medical team and let them have a go at the old guy—I mean just to get some data on these phenomena. Hell, I don't mean that there's anything *wrong* with him. Ha ha."

Hughes's assistant, Billy Steele, an Eastman dropout and would-be tenorman, shook his head and told us that Carnes had sent Cody Jones out to buy him some new records; he had instructed Cody to buy him anything he could find by Glenn Gould or Vladimir Horowitz. "The man has been listening to the piano sonatas of Alessandro Scarlatti," Billy said in the mock voice of a classical-station radio announcer. "I didn't sign up for this job to have to spend half the evening listening to goddamn Scarlatti. That is one above-average-dead dude," Billy added sadly.

The singular aspect of Carnes's altered sonic personality, as far as I was concerned, was how little contact with Thelma Watkins it was based upon. At the party, when she had said her thank-you's and good-bye's, Carnes had walked Ms. Watkins to her car. The two of them had stood out there talking for maybe five minutes—Marianne had pulled aside a curtain, and I had joined her there in the foyer to catch a glimpse of that sidewalk scene. Of course we couldn't hear what they said to each other, but we do know that their good night was formalized by a hand-shake and a belly laugh from Carnes that we heard from where we stood in the house—but not a kiss, not even a peck on the cheek.

Following the party, there had been one call, made by Carnes from his apartment phone, in which he had asked Ms. Watkins if she might consider having dinner with him, and she had said yes, but not until Friday after next—she had term papers from her seniors that were going to take up all of her time that coming weekend. He had been surprisingly cheerful in agreeing to wait so long to see her.

The philosophical question that nagged me was how a major artist like Carnes could be so profoundly affected by a woman with whom he'd exchanged fewer than five hundred words, seen no more than a couple of hours, and been intimate with only to the extent of having shaken her hand twice. Was great art really so fickle as that?

Yes seemed to be the obvious answer, and since Carnes's encounter with Thelma Watkins evidently demonstrated a fickleness of profound proportion, incumbent upon those of us involved in the project, it seemed to me, was the duty to expli-cate his experience as intelligently as possible.

We have been taught—or somehow learned—to perceive significant change in an artist's work as resulting from momen-tously traumatic life experiences. Eddie Carnes met a high school teacher at a party and shook hands good night with her; within a week, his work had changed as drastically as Picasso's movement from the "rose period" into cubism.

The practical question that nagged me was to what extent our project should involve itself with Carnes's—to phrase it crudely—love life.

Our initial agreement with Carnes was that the Project had the right to record, in aural, visual, and printed media, everything he did, everything he said, every note he played. At the time he signed the agreement—with a shaking hand but a grand flourish nevertheless—Carnes had refused even to discuss those provisions: "No problem, gentlemen," he had said. "No problem whatsoever. I just want to play my horn. And if you gentlemen want to listen in, why bless you, be my guest."

Admittedly, Carnes had changed a great deal since the day he affixed his signature to that document. Nevertheless, we were legally—if not ethically—entitled to scrutinize whatever exchanges he might have with Thelma Watkins. Indeed, we had recorded the phone call Carnes made to Ms. Watkins to ask her out to dinner, though it had not been our intention to eavesdrop on that particular conversation; our equipment had simply routinely picked it up.

However, it was not simple routine that had me pocketing the cassette of that afternoon's phone calls and taking it home with me to play for Marianne. Though I recognized this overnight borrowing of the tape as an act of questionable integrity, I needed Marianne's advice as to how to proceed at this crucial point in the Project's history. Congress was again threatening to cut the Endowment's budget, and my director was heavily involved in lobbying for his projects. The last thing he needed to know was that the Carnes Project was about to face a *romantic* problem. If push came to shove, as it might in a few months when the renewal of the Endowment's funding came up in the House, my director needed to be able to blame any errors of judgment on someone else—and in the case of the Carnes Project, that someone else was me.

Such was my thinking when I brought the recording home with me.

There is a look Marianne takes on in her professional clothing that I must say I appreciate a great deal, though I recognize that primness is a dominant theme in female attorneys' fashions. "A nun with style, that's how I'm supposed to look," Marianne has complained to me on those occasions when I have accompanied her to Taft's Corners to shop for the blazers, flannel skirts, and high-collared blouses that she is expected to wear in her office and her classroom at Georgetown Law School. Nevertheless, we both enjoy the stuffy luxuriousness of those clothes, the understated tailoring, the subtle blending of dark and darker strands of wool, the fine texture of silk and pinpoint oxford.

Around our house, though, when she comes home from the office, Marianne will frequently untuck and unbutton her blouse, will slide down and step out of her panty hose, and will sit with her feet up and her flannel skirt any old which way. Such disarray is her momentary rebellion against the strictures of her life. When she first began doing it, we were both a little surprised at how the look aroused me.

"Slatternly is apparently what I go for," I confessed to her. "What can I say?" I said.

However, consistent with our erotic history, we also discovered that in this hour of my arousal, Marianne was in the opposite state, a kind of romantic trough. She was tired and almost always at least partially angry—usually at a male colleague or a male student who had attempted some male form of bullying with her. I give Marianne credit; she had, in the past, made an effort to accommodate my desire for her during our cocktail hour, but for both of us the results had been disheartening.

So I have come to witness Marianne's quotidian dishevelment with a kind of esthetic detachment—as if I were watching a film by Truffaut in which a classically tall, thin, initially impeccable woman loosens her clothing, then sits with one foot on the floor, the other on the coffee table, her skirt at midthigh, and raises her bourbon and soda to the camera. "To the male gender—may it continue to self-destruct!" Marianne ordinarily follows her customary toast with a snort and a guffaw.

This particular evening I had the tape cued and waiting for her so that when we had settled ourselves with our drinks in the living room, all Marianne had to listen to was Carnes's phone conversation with Thelma Watkins, which, to be perfectly frank, sounded comically—embarrassingly—decorous: *". . . and I was just wondering if you might like to have dinner with me. . . ."*

"Well, Mr. Carnes, I'm very flattered that . . ."

I clicked off the machine and waited for her response. Apparently, it had been an unusually exhausting day for Marianne. She lay with both her feet resting on the sofa back, and she set the cold bottom of her glass in the center of her forehead. With her eyes closed like that, she was silent for such a while that I thought perhaps she had drifted into a nap. However, I waited her out—as over the years I have learned to do in order to make occasions for her to speak with absolute candidness. When she finally did speak, my mind had been wandering back through the archives of the history of Marianne and Henry. What she said snapped me back to the issue at hand.

"Henry, I can give you professional advice about what to do in this matter. That's the easy part. Talk to Carnes himself. Tell him what your thinking is, tell him you want to be able to demonstrate some crucial issues about the nature of the artistic process. Tell him no one's ever been able to look carefully at the way a relationship affects an artist. Blah, blah, blah. My guess is that Carnes will tell you he doesn't mind your boys carrying on business as usual.

"You'd probably also want to ask his advice on how to present the matter to Ms. Watkins. She's not likely to be enthusiastic about having her personal life incorporated into the official history of Eddie Carnes and his music. And you'll have to be scrupulous in observing whatever limitations she wants to impose on your taping.

"But I think you and I both had better recognize that we have a *personal* interest in what's happening with Eddie Carnes. Don't you think we'd better admit that to ourselves and each other? I've been thinking about it ever since we peeked at them out the window at that party. It was no mystery why you might want to keep an eye on them—part of your crazy job and all that—but I wondered what I was doing, spying on them like some dame in a James Bond movie. It disturbed me even more when I thought about it. Don't we want something out of those two people, Henry? Don't we want them to do something for us? Or don't we want what's happening between them to do something about what's not happening between us?"

Characteristic of Marianne's serious conversational style, she had refined her phrasing into an exactness that suited her. It was a quality that made her a strong attorney and an excellent law professor. She was quiet then, and I was, too, for a long while. "Yes," I said. "Yes, I see that now."

Marianne lifted her glass off her forehead and turned to face me. "Professionally, I advise you not to bring home any more tapes." Her eyes held mine for such a length of time that I came to understand what she wanted me to understand.

"But you'll understand if I choose to disregard your advice?"

"Personally, yes, I'll understand that. I was your wife before I became a lawyer. I expect I'll be your wife when I finish being a lawyer."

"And you'll understand if I happen to bring home a tape every now and then?"

She turned her face back toward the ceiling and placed the bottom of her cold glass back on her forehead. "I can get through the rest of my life without anything changing much one way or the other. I'm inclined to be a cheerful person, as you know. But I have this dread that one morning when I'm eighty years old, I'm going to wake up and realize that I've been a prisoner. I'm going to look over at you and see that you've been a prisoner, too—for years!—and that maybe we could have done something different that would have made us happier. Sometimes I think you and I traded the promise of our whole lives for what we had those first few months we were married."

"This is what people do," I said. "This is what happens. It isn't as if we don't have very rewarding lives; it isn't as if we don't enjoy each other."

Marianne sighed. "Yes, I know you're right, Henry. I'm okay, as you very well know, and I know you're fine, too. I don't mean to be whining, and I know part of it is just that it's been a long day, and my skull feels like it's going into labor. But part of this negative fantasy of mine is that after you and I have waked up and realized that we've been prisoners, the nurse or somebody is going to come in and tell us, 'Oh yeah, I forgot to tell you, you guys have been in constant pain all this time.' And then it's going to hit us, years and years of pain that we haven't even known we were experiencing. I see us both just howling."

"Yes. Maybe so," I said. "Maybe that's just how it'll be."

V

I DID IN FACT have a talk with Carnes in which I subtly attempted to convey to him that, unless he requested otherwise, we would continue our audio- and video-taping as we had been doing all along. To this day, I do not know if he understood me and gave me tacit permission to carry on or if I simply imagined his understanding and agreement while actually he was in his own world so completely that I would have had to shout into his face to get the issue across to him.

"Henry, your boys don't get in my way. I appreciate that. I appreciate that a lot." He was impatient to talk about the tape from the party, of the impromptu combo with the Marsalis brothers, to which he had been listening and about which he was excited. "Wouldn't mind for that to go into the stores," he said. "First time the five of us ever played together. Definitely something happening in those tunes. You don't hear that except when the musicians get excited about what they're hearing from each other. It's rough here and there—I like that anyway—but anybody cares about the music isn't going to be bothered. On 'Coldest Blues,' that Branford was sailing. I'd heard that Wynton's brother could play, but nobody said he could get up there like that. I even heard that those two didn't get along anymore, but I'm here to testify that their *horns* still get along just fine."

Never really unsociable, Carnes had always been generous in answering questions or trying to provide information to us. When we talked with him, we always had a sense that he was trying to give as much of himself to us as he could. But he was also a man who gave plenty of signals when it was time for a conversation to be over. Talking privately with him in the past, I had experienced a steadily increasing awareness of his desire to get back to his music. Now, even though I'd been with him for more than an hour, he seemed to want me to stay with him there in his little kitchen and to keep the conversation going.

"That white Zulu wife of yours, Henry, what did she think of that music that night? I snuck a peek at her; she looked like she was digging it; then I glanced again, and her face told me she had dropped in on the wrong planet. So I stopped looking.

Somebody like her can make me lose the changes. She say anything to you? Look like she definitely had her thoughts."

"Marianne doesn't quite know what to make of jazz, Eddie," I told him. I went on to tell him of her parents' desire for Marianne to have a practical education and a financially rewarding career. "They were determined that she not be 'tracked' into the arts just because of her gender. So they kept her from being warped one way, but the background they gave her was warped in the other direction. She never really even had a chance to hear jazz until she and I got married," I told him.

"Women." He shook his head. "I give 'em my life, but they don't even know it. I keep on telling them my story; they don't listen. Or else they hearing me better than I think they are. Maybe they hearing more than I'm telling. I don't know." The grin he gave me was classically rueful. "What do you think, Henry?"

It shocked me that he would ask what I thought. So far as I could recall, I hadn't ever seen Carnes in a questioning mode. I had come to expect him to be self-contained. He certainly wasn't a conversational bully, he wasn't insensitive, and he even seemed to be a good listener whenever anyone told him something. But at this moment I couldn't remember his ever having asked anybody a question.

"I'm not a musician, Eddie," I told him. "Or an artist of any kind. So I don't tell my story. I have to depend on guys like you to do my telling for me."

"Well, then, you in a sad way, son!" He laughed long and loud. "You let me do your telling for you, you talking about what you might not want credit for." Then, as he sat gazing at me in a very friendly and companionable way, his face changed. He turned toward that kitchen window of his that he spent ordinarily so much time staring out of. I began to have that old feeling of his wanting the conversation to be over. I stood up and stretched. I told him that I probably ought to get back to the office. I told him I'd see what I could do about getting the tape of the party combo moving toward some kind of commercial production.

"What do you think we ought to call the record, Eddie?" It wasn't really a serious question. I was already standing at the door, and I was looking for a light tone to finish up our talk.

"What should we call it?" Carnes mused. "'Back to the Kitchen'? Something like that? I don't know. I'll ask that school-teacher what she thinks we ought to call it. She and I going out on the town Friday night. I'll ask her what she thinks and let you know."

When I left him, Carnes seemed to have perked himself up with the thought of his forthcoming evening with Thelma Watkins.

VI

THERE ARE WAYS TO persuade yourself that you're not really responsible for what you're doing. Government employees know this better than people in most other professions.

The recording system in Carnes's studio and living quarters had been in place and working so long that he didn't think about it anymore, and we didn't give it much attention, either. The equipment simply kept cranking out these cassettes, which one of the Project's interns labeled and filed each morning. For it to be otherwise, someone would have to make a conscious decision to stop the procedure and turn off the equipment.

That Friday, nobody noticed anything special about what Carnes was up to, and that sly old man was successful in keeping his high spirits muted to such an extent that no one thought to tease him about his date that evening. But all day I was intensely aware of both his schedule and his mood—his glee seemed obvious to me, but I wasn't about to say anything to anybody else about it. And that evening I was the last one to leave the Project offices. Naturally, I checked to see that the taping equipment was on as usual. My guess—indeed, my hope!—was that Carnes never gave the slightest thought to the likelihood that his evening with Thelma Watkins would be recorded.

Marianne and I were scheduled for dinner out that night; she, however, called me at home to say that she needed another couple of hours at her office—she was presenting a paper on child-support guidelines at a legal educators' meeting next week. She sounded tired. We agreed we'd order pizza instead of going out. She was pleased that I wanted to wait to eat until she came home.

I'm not one of those men who's comfortable around the house by himself. It's just never been something I liked very much. I wander around, looking out this window and that, channel grazing on the TV, reading a bit of a magazine or maybe a review in the *Post* that I didn't get to that morning. I open the refrigerator and stare at the contents before I decide that I don't really want anything to eat.

If Marianne's home, I don't have a problem. I talk with her or I just sit with her—that's okay with me, being quiet while she reads—or the two of us watch TV. She's pretty calm around the house, at least she is when I'm there. Maybe she'd say the same thing about me—I must seem to her to be perfectly comfortable at home. Because that's what I am when she's in the house with me. I've never mentioned to her how antsy I am around there when she's not home. Probably I hadn't thought much about it before.

I found myself in the bedroom, standing in front of her dresser, staring into her lingerie drawer. I picked out a slip that I liked her to wear—though I'd never told her as much—very lacy and light in my hands when I unfolded it. When I held it up to the light, it was the gauzy ghost of Marianne.

I tried to imagine Marianne at home without anybody around. Surely she wouldn't do the weird routines that I found myself doing. I smiled at the idea of her opening up my underwear drawer and holding my T-shirts up to the light. Men and women are unaccountably different in their inclinations; how clearly in that moment I could see! I fixed Marianne's things as I thought I'd found them and closed the drawer, meaning, I think, to head downstairs, to pour myself a drink, and to discipline myself into reading something worthwhile.

I couldn't remember ever having thought about Marianne by herself. Plenty of times I'd imagined her in her car, driving to work or driving home or driving on trips. I'd thought about her traveling, sitting in airports, riding in taxis into other cities, always moving toward some kind of activity or group of people. Maybe when she'd been away on business trips, I'd even imagined her in hotel rooms by herself—but in that case I think I usually envisioned her calling me or calling her parents in Fredericksburg or showering and dressing to go out to dinner with her colleagues.

Why was I finding it so difficult to think about her just killing time at home, just being alone, the way I was right then? The oddest notion came to me: What difference would it make how tall Marianne was if she was home by herself? Or how blue her eyes were? Or what she looked like at all? Or how smart she was? Who would care about any of that? Even she herself wouldn't be concerned about those qualities of hers that meant so much to those of us who knew and loved her.

So then the question was, What *would* matter about her? What would be the part of herself that determined what she would do and how she would feel in that circumstance?

Did one person ever get to see what really mattered about another person?

I didn't know.

Part of what was wrong here was that I didn't like thinking about Marianne being in a circumstance that I myself was finding somewhat unpleasant at the moment. But I couldn't seem to put my finger on exactly why the idea of Marianne alone caused me such discomfort.

Sitting halfway down our staircase—just because that's where I'd stopped to sit—I almost wept at the idea or the image, whatever. Of course I didn't take myself seriously. In the past, occasionally, I'd had experiences like this, when I seemed about to be overwhelmed by powerful emotions triggered by something slight. When I cleared my head, I was certain I'd be able to focus perfectly well on Marianne's being by herself.

Carnes on the other hand was someone I'd gotten so used to thinking of as being by himself that I had trouble envisioning him being *connected*—to Thelma Watkins or to anyone else— the way I was connected to Marianne. And I wondered why that was the case. Was it because he was a musician or an artist? Did I ordinarily think of artists as being alone? Was it because Carnes was black that I so easily isolated him in my mind.

I remembered a conversation about race Carnes had had with Robin Stone, a young white tenorman who had come by the studio some months before to pay his respects. "I'll tell you what I think the basic difference is," Carnes had told Stone. "You have to think about being white about ten percent of your time, and I have to think about being black about ninety percent of mine. Everything else is pretty much the same—but that's still a pretty big difference."

This memory and these thoughts seemed about to get the best of me. I felt as guilty as if I'd been a member of the Ku Klux Klan for all these years and suddenly seen how odious it had all been. So far as I could figure it, Carnes's race had nothing to do with the ease with which I could imagine him being by himself. He was simply a man who, in the months of my acquaintance with him, stood alone in the world. Nevertheless, I felt terrible.

"Henry, what in God's name are you doing? Have you gone to bed at nine o'clock? I thought we were going to order pizza."

I was so happy Marianne had finally come home that I wasn't as embarrassed as I probably should have been about being curled up in our bed with all my clothes still on. "I just got bored without you here to talk to, darling." I threw off the covers and nearly leaped out of the bed to give her a hug. "I thought I'd take a nap while I waited for you. So I'd be good company for you when you got here."

My mood changed so drastically and so rapidly that I became almost too silly to manage ordering the pizza. Though her day had been long and extremely abrasive, Marianne was charmed by my antics. There is a reluctant smile that comes to her face that is very dear to me, that inspires me to perform like a trained bear for her, my ultimate goal being to provoke her to put her hands on her hips and say, "Now, stop it, Henry, just stop it," as she tries (and fails) to force her expression into a frown. At bedtime, we were very affectionate with each other. In my estimation, we came very close to igniting the old carnal kindling.

VII

TIMING IS THE SECRET to most issues of human relations. I suspected that I had picked up this notion from Carnes, who loved to wink at you and say, "Timing," if he had played something especially well, or on the occasion of any sort of achievement. But his one-word philosophy, or perhaps theology, also applied to failures—from dropping a glass to botching a glissando—in which case, he would shrug and shake his head and say, "Timing."

In this case, the issue was the timing of Marianne's and my hearing the tapes of Carnes's evening with Ms. Watkins—there were three cassettes, which meant there had been plenty to record. At the Project offices the next day, they had gone unheard, so far as I knew. Carnes had successfully kept his morning-after behavior sufficiently ordinary to avoid reminding anyone he'd been out the previous night. I had no idea what had transpired that evening or what Carnes's plans were for seeing Ms. Watkins again. But I knew the exact drawer in our library and the exact place in that drawer where the tapes were stored. I waited a couple of days before I found an occasion to remove them and slide them into my leather portfolio case.

I had decided against overtly announcing to Marianne what I intended to do; I had no wish to challenge her scruples—professional or otherwise—by making her decide far in advance whether or not we would hear these tapes. Instead I felt I had carried out a peripheral communication with her on the topic. I suspect that about 75 percent of what transpires between husbands and wives takes this form. Neither person actually says, "I'm going bowling tonight," or "I'm going to buy that dress I told you about," or "We'll be having Swiss Steak for dinner," but the information makes its way from one brain to the other by way of the intricate nuances that spouses have learned to send to and receive from each other.

I had asked Marianne if she had any particular plans for this Wednesday evening—and she had said no. In another conversation I had mentioned to her a raucous exuberance that had suddenly appeared in Carnes's playing—squeaks and squawks of a sort that he had eschewed his entire career up until now. And in still another exchange, this one at breakfast that very morning, I had asked Marianne if she thought Ms. Watkins was actively looking for companionship in the same way that Carnes was.

Marianne had thought about it a moment before answering. "Well, maybe not in exactly the same way. Women are not generally as goal oriented as men are, as you know, but I expect that somewhere in her consciousness there's that old, familiar biological voice whispering to her."

"You mean 'yes'?"

She sipped her coffee, leveling a stare at me over the edge of her cup. "Not exactly," she said before rising to go finish dressing for work.

So at dinner with her that evening, I suspected that at least on some level of consciousness, Marianne knew I had brought home these tapes, and I felt as antsy as Carnes must have felt the afternoon before he went out with Ms. Watkins. I must have been somewhat less successful about disguising my true state of being because as we were clearing the table, Marianne remarked, "What is it with you, Henry? You act like a kid who's planning to slip out his bedroom window after midnight."

Rather than answer her—and therefore verbalize the issues—I simply went to the dining room chair where I had put down my portfolio case, extracted the tapes, brought them back to the kitchen, and plunked the cassettes on the white countertop beside our gathering of dirty dishes. Marianne looked at them only a moment before turning her eyes to my face. We said nothing more during the several minutes it took for her to wash the dishes and me to dry them. When I glanced at her, Marianne slightly tightened her lips, a more-than-adequate communication of her feelings.

Our kitchen received extraordinary attention from the two of us that evening. We attended to the most minute details of tidiness. When there was nothing else we could do, short of pulling out the refrigerator and dusting behind it, we marched into the living room. Picking up a copy of *Family Advocate*, Marianne took her seat in one of my grandmother's high-backed wing chairs. I carried the tapes to the stereo and fast-forwarded the first one to about the point where I guessed Carnes's evening would have begun, then I had to listen a bit and fast-forward it a bit more to reach a point where I thought we should begin.

Carnes's studio and apartment microphones were voice-, or noise-, activated, a characteristic that was noticeable on the tape only when he wasn't holding a normal conversation, or playing his saxophone, or even noodling around on the piano, which he was inclined to do in the early stages of his compositions. Those phenomena it picked up and recorded with astonishing clarity and fidelity. The tiny mobile mikes we had installed in his jacket pockets were slightly more problematic, but then fidelity wasn't really an issue for what they picked up. When I finally did start the first tape and sit down to listen, Marianne and I exchanged glances. Now and then one or the other of us would inhale sharply, or say something out loud. A couple of times Marianne raised her finger to her lips to shush me, and more than once one of us would try to talk to the other while the tape was playing.

"Yeah, I guess this is the place" was the observation that cued me to begin the tape. It was followed by the slamming of the car door, presumably behind Carnes as he turned toward Ms. Watkins's house or apartment, and by the muted cadence of his footsteps. There was a background noise that rose in pitch as Carnes's footsteps changed their pace and pitch—apparently from his climbing a short flight of steps. I informed Marianne that the noise was the rumbling of Carnes's belly. "He's anxious," I told her.

No trace of a smile came to Marianne's lips.

Carnes both knocked and rang a doorbell; still there was a bit of a wait—during which Carnes paced inside a hallway or foyer—before a door unlocked and opened. *"Good evening, Mr. Carnes. I thought perhaps you might have trouble finding—"*

He interrupted her. *"Ed, or Eddie, please, Ms. Watkins, or I guess I mean Thelma, unless you'd rather I didn't call you by your first—"*

"No, it's fine, I mean—" There were some door-locking noises followed by feet shuffling, then making their way back down the short flight of steps.

"Well, then, we should—"

"Ed?"

"Or Eddie. Whichever. Thelma."

"Yes, Thelma."

Carnes cleared his throat. *"This car's what they give me whenever I want to go anywhere, Thelma. They give me this driver, too. I guess they think I can't drive. Maybe I can't, I don't know. Been a long time. My license ran out when I lived in Sweden. Anyway, if it was my car I was coming to pick you up in, it wouldn't be this one. Here you go."*

Apparently he shut the door on Ms. Watkins while she was asking him what sort of a car he would have picked her up in if it had been his own.

"Timing," he muttered to himself while he walked around to the other door. I could see him shaking his head and taking on his rueful expression. *"Do better,"* he instructed himself as he opened the door on his side.

"I guess it would be one of those Saabs. I got to liking those cars when I was over there. I think I wrecked one of them one night. Meant to be backing up and drove it right into somebody's front porch. But if I ever get me another car, it'll be a Saab, dark red, and leather seats, with one of those new stereos makes you think you in a studio when you're driving along. That's what I'd bring to your door, Thelma."

"Nice car. That would be a nice car, Ed." She would be nod-

ding at him, encouragingly. "Eddie *maybe. Try* Eddie *and see if it sounds all right.* Ed *makes me think I need to sit up straight.*"

"Eddie *makes me think I need to send you to the principal's office. Should we go back to* Mr. Carnes?"

"*Oh, no, mercy, let's don't go back to that, Thelma. I'll see if I can get along with* Ed. *Sitting up a little straighter won't hurt me. Just don't send me down to that principal's office.*" The two of them laughed as if this were the most amusing occasion of their adult lives.

At this point Marianne said, "Why are we listening to this, Henry? I know I'm the one who said we wanted to. Did I say why we wanted to? They're so—I don't know what they are. But this embarrasses me."

I knew that Marianne didn't want or need an answer from me. I nodded at her. I knew she understood that I, too, was painfully conflicted about what we were doing. And I took note of the fact that, in spite of her protest, she hadn't actually asked me to turn off the tape. I said nothing.

"*So you're a teacher. Wil says that even when you were a little girl and his family came to visit yours, you liked to correct his English.*"

Ms. Watkins laughed sociably. "*Yes, I did like that—Mother let me get by with it because I was an only child, and she thought it wouldn't harm Wil anyway. I did love improving my little cousin Wil. Perhaps you have noticed that Wil speaks a very clear* standard English; he has used that ability to his advantage, and he has his cousin to thank for it."

"I didn't finish high school."

"I know that, Ed."

There was a lengthy pause before Carnes spoke again. *"How you going to keep from correcting my English? We got a whole dinner to get through, just the two of us."*

Again there was that polite laugh from Ms. Watkins, but within it there was a note of warmth, so clearly present that Marianne and I widened our eyes at each other to remark it. I could just see Ms. Watkins—I think I began to think of her as *Thelma* in exactly this moment—reaching over and patting his hand as she spoke, and Carnes's clasping her hand and holding onto it.

"Ed, my cousin says that he has personally known only one or two persons in the world as intelligent as you are. I don't know if you know just how devoted to you my cousin is; to be around you, he'd be happy just to stand by your side all day and hand you toothpicks when you needed them."

"Maybe you better set him straight, just like in the old days."

This time the note her laugh sounded was one of sorrow, an almost harmonic response to the humorously rueful tone of Carnes's voice. *"One thing I have learned. My cousin's judgment of people is very precise. Perhaps he has told you about my former husband, the little-beloved Nelson Watkins? When I took that man to meet Wil, Wil hadn't been around him five minutes before he took me aside and said, 'Cuz, I know he's being nice to you, but that man will do you some harm. Don't trust him.' I'm sorry to say that I told my little cousin to relax, to try to put his racism aside and to look at Nelson for what he was. If I had listened to Wil then, I'd have saved myself fifteen years of trouble. Fifteen long years of trouble."* And now Thelma's laugh sounded the bitter joy of saying good-bye to the trouble.

"So this is where you're taking me to dinner? Well, I'm very flattered. I've heard it's just the place."

"I don't know anything about it." The car door slammed, and there was a pause with some pacing while Carnes came around to Thelma's side to open her door. *"I just asked Cody Jones. He eats out a lot, knows all the fancy places. Cody said this was where I should take you."*

There followed a bit of murmuring, pacing, door opening, maneuvering, and then a background noise of voices, clinking glasses, and silverware. Carnes was apparently expected at this place because he and Thelma were seated very quickly—for days afterward Marianne and I tried to guess which restaurant it might have been, but we couldn't even come up with a likely possibility. They began studying their menus right away, which was interesting because Carnes immediately asked Thelma to pick out what he should eat. *"I never could order anything I wanted from a restaurant menu. I gave up on that years ago.*

What looks great to me on the menu isn't what I want when they set it in front of me. Been that way since I was a kid."

Thelma ordered a Chateaubriand for the two of them, and she persuaded Carnes to try a bottle of sparkling cider. When it came, she proposed a toast: *"To music."*

The clinking of their glasses was followed by a significant pause, during which I knew that, just as I was, Marianne was struggling to envision the nature of the interaction between Carnes and Thelma. It struck me then how such moments as these determined individual destinies. One of them could have seen in the other's slight relaxing of facial muscles a significant opening up of the self, could have sensed the other's offering of vast resources of intrigue and understanding. One of them could have decided—intelligently or stupidly—that the other would be endlessly engaging.

VIII

Mr. Carnes—Ed. I'm sorry. Let me start over again. Ed. I appreciate your taking me out. This is a rare occasion for me, and I understand that you, too, haven't had much of a social life either since you've been here in the Washington area. I'm curious about the man whose shadow my cousin has decided to stand in as long as you'll let him. I wonder if you'd mind telling me about yourself."

"You already know more than most people do."

"I do know some things. Wil has told me a lot."

"I told you some, too, Thelma. The other night when the boys and I were playing at the party. I told you all the really important stuff right then. Told you so much you had to step back in the kitchen."

"I'm not a musician, Ed. Am I blushing? Well, maybe I did notice how intensely you were playing. But I didn't have any way to know what I was hearing, or what you might have wanted me to hear. Listening to you with those people all around me, I felt uncomfortable. That's why I had to leave the room. I needed to sit down by myself for a minute. I could still hear you from in there. As I say, I'm not a musician. All the family talent for music went to Wil. But even if I could have understood what you were playing, I'd still like to hear what you'd choose to tell me face to face like this. In plain English, as we say. Whatever you want me to know."

"What I want you to know?"

"Yes."

"What I want you to know, and I can't use my horn to tell it to you. Well now. Do you give your students this kind of assignment?"

"No, Ed." Her voice was very soft. "This is an assignment for a grown-up."

Their waiter came to serve them something—salad, I supposed—the interlude of which would give him time to gather his thoughts. I understood what must have been perfectly evident to Carnes: His future was about to be determined by what he told this woman. I found myself weirdly cheering him on: *Talk for your life, Eddie!* I nearly said out loud.

"Thelma, I'll take you at your word and tell you what I can. It may not be anything you want to hear. In a few weeks I'll be *sixty-one years old. I'm a drunk who has the good luck not to be drinking right now. But I'm not to be trusted in that regard—I don't trust myself, which is why I'm keeping myself away from my old pal Mr. Booze right now.*

"I'm somebody who always wanted to be close to somebody—always wanted to be close to a woman, I should go ahead and say, because that's how it's been. When I was little, I was what they used to call a mama's boy, but my mama was a schoolteacher, and so she had work to do. She used to have to run me out of the house, I hung around her so close. So all my life I did a lot of chasing women. Trying to get back in that house and hang around with Mama, you know. Then when one of these women seemed like she wanted to let me hang around her all the time, I had to run myself out of the house. Wanted to hang around with Mama but didn't know how to do it. Couldn't let myself be close to anybody.

"I don't know why that was the way things went; it just was. With the result being what you see sitting right here in front of you, somebody so totally by himself he wants to break your heart every time he picks up a horn. Anybody who hears me—man or woman—I want them to be thinking, 'Man, that Eddie Carnes, he must be the one I've been wanting to meet all my life. That Eddie Carnes must be a man with a hundred-and-ten-percent platinum soul.' Fact is, over the years, plenty of people—men and women—have stepped forward to try to give me exactly what my

horn told them I wanted. 'I accept your adoration,' I say, 'but it's not quite enough. I have to have more.' So then I stash away that little offering of adoration and go on playing, trying to build up this store of love, trying to warehouse what people are so kind as to bring me.

"There's got to be something on the other side of that. I have to tell you the truth. I'm a lot better musician than I deserve to be, and I think there has to be some kind of reason for that. I'm not even close to religious, but I can't believe that I got born into this world with the privilege of being able to play beautiful music just to be able to get a lot of people to testify that they think I have a beautiful soul.

"If it don't come out to more than that, then music ain't what I think it is. And all those people whose music I love so much just threw their lives away. If it don't come out to more than that, then all music is is what you hear at the grocery store, some bunch of union-scale fiddle players sawing on a Beatles song to make you buy more margarine.

"Here's a little story for you, Thelma, a little story for the two of us, since you asked me to tell you whatever I wanted to about myself, and I'm taking you up on your dare, I'm accepting your invitation.

"In my sixth grade, there was this thing that started at recess with somebody rolling down a hillside. I don't remember who it was, or even if it was a boy or a girl. It doesn't matter. Somebody else saw it and went rolling down, too. Soon enough, all of us boys and girls, or at least a lot of us, began rolling down in turns.

"It must have been springtime, because that's the weather I remember, some sweetness in the air and just warm enough to take your jacket off after you'd rolled down the hill a couple of times. The slope was right at the edge of the schoolyard, so it felt like we were doing something away from school, something private, just among ourselves. The teachers didn't have anything to do with it, you know what I mean?

"One afternoon, a boy rolled into a girl—I seem to have in mind that it was James Blair rolling into Marilyn Scott—and the two of them commenced tussling and giggling. When they stopped rolling down at the bottom of the hill, they picked themselves up, walked back up the hill, and repeated the whole thing.

"Soon enough, the rest of us were imitating them. It had this boy-girl requirement to it that wasn't like anything else we did. The pairs of us just clicked into place, like each one of us had been waiting through those first six grades of school to make a move on that particular girl or that particular boy. After a while what had been just some children rolling down the hill had evolved into coeducational wrestling matches with a rolling component to them.

"I don't think many of us knew what we were doing. But we damn sure knew we liked it and meant to keep on doing it. It was sort of a competition, girls versus boys, but it was also like a

project you had to work on with each other; you had to cooperate.
I mean it was strange. It was like playing and it was like fighting,
which we understood well enough. But there was this new
dimension to it. To make it work—to make it feel good—we
needed each other, and we had to admit to each other that we
needed each other. We had a couple of days of recesses to work on
it and refine the procedure, as it were.

"It got to be our passion. Kids from the other grades would
come out and watch us, but we had claimed the hill, and we
didn't let anybody do it except just us sixth-graders who had
been in on it from the start. It was wild out there. Girls stopped
worrying about whether or not their dresses came up. Boys' shirts
started coming off. People's clothes got ripped.

"You can figure out what would have happened. Just about
the time things were about to go completely out of control, our
teacher, Miss Whitt, and our principal, Mr. Jackson, made us
stop. When we stayed and tried to do it after school, on our own
time, a couple of us got paddled the next day; a couple more of us
were sent home. No matter how much we wanted to do our thing
out there, we had no choice but to give it up.

"That's the outside of that story. The inside of it is what
happened between me and Diana Childress. Diana was tall and
skinny—the way a lot of girls are at that age—and she had the
darkest skin of anybody in my sixth-grade class. Her mother was
Haitian. She had this proper little accent whenever she said any-

72

thing, which wasn't that often. Maybe it was just quiet-person's accent, I don't know. Anyway, she was mostly a fierce and silent girl. I think that's what I liked most about Diana, that fierceness that seemed like it could break out of her any moment, though I don't remember her ever losing her temper.

"She wore white socks and bright blue and yellow cotton dresses, ironed very nicely I guess by her mama, with the skirt hemmed to just below her knees. Diana kept her hair done up just so and held her head in this prideful way. Scary enough to make us boys keep our distance. But I'll confess that I'd had my eye on that girl ever since she came to our school in third grade. Maybe I thought I saw her looking at me, too, not often but just every now and then.

"When that time came, in the rolling down the playground hillside, when the boys and girls paired off the way we did, it didn't take half a second for Diana and me to find each other. She was just there in front of me, or I was there in front of her, like we had known all along that something like this was going to happen. We had hold of each other's shoulders; we were glaring into each other's faces. Then we were just gone down that hillside. Just gone!

"I can see us now as clearly as if somebody had taken a home movie of us, Diana Childress and Eddie Carnes rolling down the hill at recess, wrestling and grunting and maybe laughing, I don't know. Soon as we got to the bottom, we were up and running to the top and grabbing hold of each other by the shoulders and arms and falling down to the ground and rolling down the hill again.

"All we ever had to say to each other was 'Get up, fool!' or 'Like this, try it like this!' or 'Hurry!' It was like she and I had this desperate errand we had to carry out, again and again.

"When it was over, I mean to tell you, it was all over. Diana and I were not the ones who got paddled or the ones who got sent home to tell our parents what we'd been up to. Compared to the others in our class, we were probably among the least indecent. I don't remember Diana's dresses coming up very much because her mama had hemmed them all down so low anyway. And I certainly kept my shirt on, didn't even dream of taking it off. But maybe it would have been better if we had been among the punished ones. Because we were definitely among the casualties.

"Over the years Mister Negative has come to visit me plenty of times—and I know I don't have to tell you about it because you ain't been attending no lifetime tea party yourself—but I'd put down the end of that hillside wrestling as one of my all-time saddest things.

"It wasn't even how terrible I felt just by myself. It was how I knew Diana felt. We didn't talk about it—couldn't really talk about it, didn't have the words even for ourselves, let alone for each other. But when I'd look at her in class or out at recess by the swings or wherever, I just knew what we'd lost. I could feel it in *my body, and I could see it in Diana's body.* Diminished *is what we were! Less than we had been!*

"Glaring at each other, wrestling, going at each other, and working with each other all at the same time—teeth and elbows and legs and bellies and all our muscles—we had been glorious!

"Then they took it away.

"Or we lost it. I don't know. We were just children.

"But I have to tell you, Thelma. That rolling down the hill with Diana Childress was the thing for me. It beat the hell out of hanging around the dining room table trying to get Mama's attention. If somebody came up to me right this minute and said, 'Eddie, you'll have to give up sex for the rest of your life, but you can go back to rolling down the hillside of Thibault Elementary School of Buffalo, New York, with Diana Childress whenever you want to,' I'd say, 'You got yourself a deal.'

"Nobody was ever so *there* with me as that girl—nothing but the naked truth of her present in those blazing eyes and flared nostrils and hard little shoulders and arms. She and I wanted to rip each other's insides out and crawl up inside each other. Our bodies were these huge stones that we were striking against each other, making fiery sparks all around ourselves, trying to kill each other and bring each other back to life all at the same time. Anything I ever had with anybody after that— friendship or love or sex or whatever—was never more than just—Carnes cleared his throat and went on. "I guess I just *talked myself out of your good graces, didn't I, Thelma? I didn't know it was going to come out like that. Happens when you try to improvise outside the changes. Got to go where it takes you. Sorry. Guess I'm just wasting your time, huh?*

"*But it's better that you know. No matter what the song is, my song has two parts to it. The first part is that I rolled down the hill with Diana Childress. The second part is that they made us stop rolling down the hill. No matter what you hear me playing, that's what I'm playing. 'Song in Two Parts,' by Eddie Carnes.*"

IX

"WHAT BOYS AND GIRLS did together, Ed, wasn't anything I knew about in sixth grade. I was one of those slow-to-mature girls. I wore glasses, read three and four books a day, got straight A's, didn't see what there was about boys, especially sixth-grade boys, that could hold anybody's attention.

"Though they were fifteen years apart in age, both my parents grew up right here in Washington, graduated from Howard, then took government jobs. So we lived in a nice neighborhood, we had nice things, and everybody treated us with respect. We were all three light skinned and very proper people. I couldn't help thinking I was better than most of the kids at my school, because they treated me like I was better than they were. They *very politely left me alone except to ask for my help with their homework or for an answer on a quiz. Until I went to college, I didn't have any friends, didn't even know what it felt like to have a close friend.*

"I was a very serious child, and I loved my parents. I know that sounds simpleminded, but, really, it was the single most important thing in my life when I was growing up. Maybe most kids love their parents, but the difference was that I knew I loved mine. I was an only child. They treated me like I was their reason for being in this world.

"That age difference between my father and my mother was something I was very aware of when I was growing up. It was as if my father had come from another world. He was very handsome, very well dressed. He wore dark suits and ties and these beautiful starched white shirts. Wing-tip shoes that he shined every morning. When he retired from the Treasury Department, he was a GS-14, quite a position for a black man to hold at that time. Everything he did, every word he spoke, was very deliberate, very thought out. And he adored me.

"It's taken me years to know how unusual a man he was, how disciplined he must have had to be. He was formal with my mother but very thoughtful. Even when just the three of us were having dinner on a weeknight, he waited for her and held her chair to seat her at the dinner table. To any questions she asked him about even the slightest little thing, he gave her very complete

answers. Her frustration with him was sometimes evident to me, but I never saw my father lose control of himself. I never saw him act other than kindly to my mother. I was the witness to my father's devotion to my mother.

"She is still alive—just turned seventy and in very good health, thank you. But it's not as easy for me to see her objectively and describe her as it is him. My father died eleven years ago this August; I have a very settled view of him, a kind of official portrait, every detail of which I hold vividly in mind, because it never changes.

"My mother and I still have a lot going on between us. Even today—even though I'm old enough to have grandchildren—I still feel my mother wanting me to do this, not wanting me to do that. I don't ask her what she thinks, and she rarely tells me; nevertheless, I don't ever make an important decision without considering what her opinion of it would be. Even having dinner with you here tonight, Ed, yes, it's true. And I won't tell you what I imagine my mother's opinion of you would be. But let's just say—

Here the first tape abruptly ended. I was ready to sit and talk a bit with Marianne before starting up the second one, but when I kept sitting still in the silence, Marianne gave me an impatient look. "More?" I asked her.

"What do you think?" I thought her tone was more brittle than the occasion called for. Nevertheless, I walked over, changed the cassettes, and started up the tape number two.

"—don't want to make her sound so bad. She had—and still has—the kind of pretensions that a lot of well-to-do white ladies of her day had. Not that many black women can afford to have the view of life she holds. At the same time, she's an extremely kind and decent person. Though she occasionally resented the bond between my father and me, she has never been anything other than considerate of me.

"She was a young woman of uncommon beauty.

"From the time she turned fourteen, people stared at her. People—white and black—treated her like royalty. Strangers expected her to be a famous singer or movie star just because she had such a remarkable face. So from early on in her life, it must have been very hard for her not to think of herself as a privileged person. She *was* privileged.

"You see, most of us have the experience of wanting more than we actually get—that's just the natural circumstance for most human beings. But my mother always had more than she wanted—more love, more attention, more praise, more success. She was always turning away things that other people would have killed for—especially the attentions of men.

"When she was growing up, she had her pick of what she used to call the eligible bachelors. She chose my father, who was older but nevertheless eligible and so desirable that he was beyond everybody else's wildest dreams. But my mother must not have seen him as anything more than she deserved. After all, in choosing him, she had had to give up a number of handsome, charming, successful young men. There was no way for her to see him other than as one among many. Modest as she tried to be, my mother could see my father only as the lucky one and herself as the one who had, however willingly, sacrificed many other possibilities for his sake.

"The informing image of my childhood is seeing my mother smile shyly at someone who has approached her, taking my father's arm, and turning her face toward his suit jacket—shielding herself from some unwanted attention by demonstrating that she was the wife of this dignified and formidable older man. My mother turned away from the attention people offered her all the time: I was aware of that from earliest childhood.

"I wish I could say that's all there is to it.

"At that time—1958, 1959, I think it would have been—my mother was a research officer at Health, Education, and Welfare. Her job was to gather statistics from all over the country and to help prepare statistical reports on the nation's schools. Her boss was a white man named Anthony Pritchett, for whom she'd worked from her first day of government service.

"Anthony Pritchett had a passionate commitment to racial integration; he had worked his way up in the bureaucracy to an associate directorship; and like just about everybody else, he thought the world of my mother. He was a bachelor with an Ivy League education, a very witty and stylish man, the kind of *person who's attracted to Washington and who usually does very well here. Over the years he'd become a friend of my parents. He'd come to our house for dinner, or else he'd take us out to dinner. Almost always he'd have some very articulate date, never a beautiful woman but always somebody with a lot of personality, somebody who'd impress you with her bright way of talking."*

Marianne caught my eye and nodded at me. I started to ask her what she meant, but I didn't want to interfere with what Thelma was telling.

"Though he never said so and though he obviously respected the man, I'm pretty certain my father had decided that Anthony Pritchett was homosexual. There was a certain amount of putting up with Mr. Pritchett that we all three understood we had to do because he was my mother's boss and because he was somebody who really was doing a lot 'for colored people.' Anthony Pritchett needed to present himself in Washington society as somebody who had Negro friends. We served that function for him—even I was aware of it—though of course he was extremely thoughtful of us, more thoughtful than he would have been if we'd been white.

"Anthony Pritchett owned a dark green Mercedes convertible, just about the most elegant car in all of Washington, maybe in all of the country in those days. He kept it polished on the outside and immaculate on the inside. It was this aspect of our friendship with him that my father and I agreed we most

appreciated, getting to ride in that lovely car when he took us out to dinner.

"One day I came home from school early—there was a teacher's meeting one Friday afternoon that I had forgotten to tell my mother about—and that green Mercedes was parked about a block and a half away from our house. That was the year I had begun riding city buses home by myself. I hadn't seen my coming home a couple of hours early as a problem; I had my own house key; I was used to letting myself in the house early and waiting an hour or two for my mother to come home. She'd worked out an arrangement with Mr. Pritchett regularly to take work home with her so that she could come home early to be with me. I'd simply have to wait for her a bit longer than I usually did.

"Walking down the street from the bus stop to my house, I passed that green Mercedes, and I said to myself, 'Oh, that's Mr. Pritchett's car.' Seeing it made me happy, reminding me of the way my father always shook his head and grinned politely at Mr. Pritchett about how pretty his car was whenever it was parked in our driveway.

"The closer I got to home, the more reluctant I became to go on. By the time I turned the corner and could see our house, my feet were dragging, and my whole body felt heavy, as if somebody had opened it up and dumped in a load of wet cement. But my brain still wasn't accepting the message. I kept walking, slower and slower.

"Nobody was home—no lights were on in our living room, as there would have been if either of my parents was there. The curtains in the upstairs bedrooms were slightly open, as we kept them during the day when we were not there. My father's car was not in the driveway. I was seeing exactly what I should have been seeing. This was where I lived. Here was where I was going to cross the street and walk up the driveway and go around to the back door. . . .

"But I wasn't able to make the turn. My body kept me walking on past the house. As I remember it now, my mind was even sort of protesting, saying, Hey, what are you doing? What's wrong with you? Where are you going?

"I kept staring back even after I had walked past it, and here is what haunts me still. A curtain moved in my parents' bedroom, as if someone had been standing there watching me walk past and wanted to keep an eye out for where I was going. I'm almost certain I saw the slightest little move of that curtain, as if someone had hooked it back with a finger. But even a moment afterwards, I was wondering if I had actually seen it.

"If a little thing like that happens, something that can't leave any evidence, then it's just so easy to doubt it. Worse still, somewhere along the line I also began doubting that the Mercedes I had passed by a couple of blocks back was Mr. Pritchett's car, or even that I passed a green Mercedes convertible.

"Nothing ever happened to confirm or deny what some

essential part of me was pretty certain had happened, that Mr. Pritchett had brought my mother home and that they had taken some trouble to disguise the fact that they were in our house together.

"I walked down the street a couple of blocks to a park where my father had often taken me as a small child. There were swings there, seesaws, crude merry-go-rounds, and structures for little kids to climb. It probably wasn't safe for me to be there by myself, but I wasn't thinking about that—or wasn't, really, thinking about anything. Something seemed to have switched my brain off, except for the part of it I needed to move my body around. I fooled around aimlessly for a while in the completely empty playground. Then I sat in a swing with my book bag in my lap until it was the usual time for me to be walking home. Then I walked home.

"When I unlocked the back door and stepped inside our kitchen, I could feel my life—my old life—tugging on me. Something inside me was desperately struggling to take up just where I'd left off and sit down at the kitchen table with a glass of milk and half a dozen Fig Newtons and get started on my math homework. The whole kitchen seemed to be telling me that that's what I should do, just wipe out of my mind Mr. Pritchett's car and the moving curtain, just pick up my life and go on with it.

"So I spread out all my stuff on the table and even took a glass down from the cabinet. But I couldn't let go of what I

thought I'd seen. Even though the weather was warm enough—
it was early fall—I'd picked up a little chill from being out on
that playground all that time. And so I told myself that I'd just
walk around the house a bit until I warmed up. What I did, of
course, was walk straight upstairs to my parents' bedroom and
check it out.

"*Nothing was different—not the bed, my parents' dressers*
and bedside tables, their clothes in their closet, not the slightest
little thing. I even stepped over to the window where I thought I'd
seen the curtain move. I stood there and hooked it with my fin-
ger. Nothing in that room told me that there'd been anybody
there since early that morning.

"*In the hallway, something turned me toward what we*
called the sewing room, though the only sewing my mother had
done in there in my whole lifetime was fixing a button back onto
the sleeve of my father's suit jacket. It wasn't a room that any of
the three of us ever had a reason to enter. Since we always kept
the door closed, I went for long periods of time forgetting that it
was even a part of our house.

"*Ed, I've already told you I was a naive child. I possessed*
only the vaguest notions of what sex was all about or of how
most grown-up men and women conducted themselves. We had
no TV. We almost never went to the movies—when we took
family outings, we went to cultural or educational events. The
books I read were on the order of Anne of Green Gables *and*

Little Women. *How my parents talked, how my parents dressed, what my parents ate, and how my parents behaved with each other and with me—those were the topics in which I had expertise. But something made me walk into that room where the instant I stepped inside I knew that my mother had been with Mr. Pritchett not more than an hour before. It was warm in there, and there was a scent that I understood as if a scientist had dissected it for me: my mother's bath soap and Mr. Pritchett's cologne.*

"*Afternoon sunlight streamed through the window while I stood there in a kind of trance.*

"*When I heard—or rather sensed—my mother's footsteps walking up the driveway toward the back door, I slipped out of the sewing room and down the hall to the bathroom. As I knew she would, my mother called to me, and I shouted back to her that I was in the bathroom. After a while, I flushed the toilet and washed my hands and came downstairs. She was waiting for me, just as I knew she would be—it's uncanny how well kids and their parents know each other, and mine and I knew each other about ten times better than most. She was sitting at the kitchen table, looking over my sheet of math problems while she waited for the water to boil for her after-work cup of tea.*"

For a few moments Carnes and Thelma were beset with waiters clearing their table, asking them how their meal had been, offering them coffee and a chance to see the dessert menu.

But Thelma began speaking again so soon that I understood she felt some urgency about finishing her story.

"*My mother and I talked—and even argued a bit—exactly the way we always did in that ninety minutes or so we had to ourselves, between her coming home and my father's coming. It was an afternoon similar to hundreds of previous afternoons we'd spent together, nothing different.*

"*Except that I was pretending I knew nothing whatsoever about what I thought I knew about. And my mother, almost certainly, was pretending that she hadn't done anything unusual earlier that day. Sometimes, when I think about this part of that day, it disturbs me more than any of it. My mother and I were each putting on an act for the other. My mother might even have seen me walking past the house and known that I suspected her of something wrong. Maybe we each knew that the other knew something. Whatever was the case, my mother revealed nothing in what she said to me or in how she behaved in my presence.*

"*She did such a good job of carrying out our usual conversational ritual that I began to doubt all of it again, despite what the sewing room had so clearly told me. A smell is the easiest thing in the world to imagine, I told myself. And just before bedtime that evening, I found a moment when I could peek into that room without my parents knowing it. It was cool in there by then, and it smelled the way it always did, kind of dank and inhospitable. With the overhead light on, the old sofa in there* looked like the last place in the world you'd want to sit down. My mother and Mr. Pritchett couldn't possibly have gone in there. They couldn't possibly have come to our house that afternoon. My mother couldn't possibly have gone into her own bedroom, hooked back the curtain with her finger to watch me walking past the house and staring back at it on my way to the playground. I had made it all up in my mind.

"If I am understanding you correctly, Ed, you are telling me that your life was powerfully affected by something you came to know in the act of rolling down the hillside with your classmate Diana Childress. It was a certainty of experience that served as a kind of reference point for your later experiences with the opposite sex.

"What I think I mean for you to understand from my little story is that the opposite was—is—the case with me. Essentially, I came not to know something—or I came to unknow something. A permanent piece of doubt was installed into my perception of how men and women behave with each other.

"With every couple I have ever known or seen or read about, I have suspected one of them of having betrayed the other. But it can't even be as simple as that: I even have to doubt my suspicion because I could have been completely wrong about my mother.

"Either way it was, I have this dreadful understanding of her. If she had an affair with Anthony Pritchett, I know what her thoughts and feelings must have been—I don't condemn her for it, though I know it would have crushed my father if he had found out about it. On the other hand, if nothing ever happened between my mother and Mr. Pritchett, I understand that perfectly well, too. She loved my father, I don't doubt that."

Carnes spoke up, which surprised both Marianne and me: He had been silent for such a length of time. "Why don't you ask your mama? She'd probably tell you. Maybe she even wants you to know."

Thelma didn't answer him right away. When she did speak, it was evident that she was thinking hard about the question: "If she did have an affair with Anthony Pritchett, I can't stand to know it—and I can't stand for her to know that I know it. The other would be fine—if she didn't have the affair. I would have no problem with that. But I can't take a chance by asking her. It's a doubt that I can't do without, however debilitating it may have been for me. However debilitating it may be."

There was another long pause before Carnes spoke again, his voice grainy, a soft rasp: "So here we are."

"Here we are. Here we are, indeed. With what we have brought with us."

X

"DEATH BY CHOCOLATE OKAY with you? I think I'd have to order it no matter what it was. "

"Death by Chocolate is fine with me, Ed. I'm sure it'll be good. You go ahead and order it and ask them to bring us two forks. But holding hands on a first date is not a good idea. My mother offered me that advice in 1964. She said it leads to what comes next—and to what comes after that."

"Ah yes, your mother. But we know about her, don't we? And what comes next is just a sweet little glide of these educated fingers down the inside of your arm. Like this."

"Why, Eddie, I'm surprised at you. I'm going to have to send you down to that principal's office after all. Are you forgetting *about all this luggage we brought with us to the restaurant?"*

"I told you a story. You told me a story. You ever been to the opera, Thelma? Way they do it there, the tenor sings his solo, the soprano sings hers, and then they sing the duet. That's where we are right now. I sang, you sang; now it's time for us to sing."

"Well, sir, I have indeed been to the opera—just enough to know how the opera always turns out. So if we're going to sing a duet, it's not going to be that same old one, the well-known my-place-or-your-place-and-please-let's-hurry-up-before-you-find-out-something-terrible-about-me-or-I-find-out-something-horrible-about-you. Besides that, I listened to your story. Did you listen to mine?"

"You telling me you don't trust me?"

"I'm telling you I don't trust you just like you told me no matter what I do, I can't live up to that skinny little girl you rolled down the hill with in sixth grade."

Marianne responded to this remark of Thelma's with a quick exclamatory pulling down of her chin.

"I don't think you understand, Thelma. We told each other those things. Takes all the harm out to tell it."

"On the contrary. It puts all the harm right up here on the table so that we can examine it carefully."

"So all right. So all right. I see you saying you don't trust me or yourself or even old Mr. Love himself. I see that, all right. I'm not running away from it. You running away from a skinny little

thing like Diana Childress?"

There were a couple of beats of silence before Thelma answered. *"No, Ed, I'm not running away. And I know you aren't. But that doesn't mean we have to run in the other direction, either."*

"Just tell me what direction we running in, lady. That's all I want to know. "

"Well, sir, I hate to tell you, but we're not running. At least I'm not. I don't know in what direction we're moving, but I know I'm taking my time."

"Long as we getting there, I don't mind the speed."

"May not be any there. *May not even be any* we."

"You too hard, lady. You just too damn difficult!"

"You give up?"

"No."

"Then my level of difficulty must not be beyond your abilities."

"So tell me what comes next. I got it straight what doesn't come next. What does?"

"You and your driver take me home. You walk me to my door, where we may have, if we choose, a very pleasant goodnight kiss. Then your driver takes you home. "

"Then what?"

"Then I'm going to call you in a week or two and invite you out to dinner."

"*You taking me out to dinner?*"

"*If you accept my invitation. That's how we do things these days. You take me out; I take you out.*"

"*So all right. Then what?*"

"*Then I will probably ask you to tell me something else about yourself.*"

"*'Nother story?*"

As Carnes clearly was, I was a bit exasperated with Thelma, too.

"*Another story, yes. And then if you ask me to, I might tell you one, too.*"

"*All right. All right. How long does this go on?*"

"*How long does what go on?*"

"*Going out. Trading stories.*"

"*Going out I don't know about. Trading stories I think has to keep going. When I don't want to hear what you have to tell me or when you don't want to hear what I have to tell you, then our friendship will, as they say, have reached a natural conclusion.*"

"*How about if I just play my horn for you?*"

"*I would like that very much, but I'm afraid that when I ask you, you're still going to have to tell me about yourself. If I were a musician, we could use our instruments to communicate with each other. Since I'm not, you're still going to have to talk to me. I need your words, sir.*"

"*This might not work out, Thelma. I might run out of words.*"

"*Yes, that's right, it might not work out. You might run out of wanting to hear what I have to tell you, too.* "

"*Or you might.*"

"*Or I might.*"

"*Be simpler for us just to go to my house and hit the sheets. Get up in the morning and take inventory.*"

"*No, that would be far too complicated for me. Maybe if we were young and didn't know very much, we could do that and not be harmed by it. I'm not going to be combing the knots out of my hair in your bathroom mirror in the morning, I'm sorry. We're too mature to behave like that, Ed. We have to do something else.* "

"*No end to the penalties of old age.*"

"*No end to the penalties. Yes, that's right.*"

Carnes and Thelma were laughing and apparently getting up from their table when Marianne suddenly stood up and walked over to the stereo to turn it off. "I'm ashamed of myself for having listened to that."

I shrugged, but she wasn't paying any attention to me. She strode back to the wing chair and flounced down. "No, I'm not at all ashamed of myself for having listened to it," she said. Then she flashed her eyes at me as if I'd accused her of having done something terrible. "She's a very refreshing woman. You and I both could learn something from her, Henry."

"And not from him?"

"In this situation, he's your classic testosterone-motivated male. She, on the other hand, is worth paying attention to. She's just as romantic as women have always been, but she's taken charge of her biological destiny. She's insisting on the value of intelligence and mutual personal inquiry and revelation as legitimate elements of courtship."

Marianne paused a moment, as if she were gathering her thoughts, her energy—even her anger—to go on. But then something in her face changed completely. She was looking at me as if she had been pulled into a trance that permitted her to see straight through my skull. "So what do you think, Henry?" she asked, her voice much softer. "What are they going to do?"

"You're asking me what they're going to do?" I really was taken aback. "It's perfectly evident that they're going to do exactly what Thelma said they were going to do. She's asserted herself. She's taken charge. She's a smart lady, and she's already explained to him why she's wary. Carnes has got himself a good-night kiss coming. That's it."

"Maybe."

"Maybe?"

"Things go the way they go, Henry. I know this from my single-women colleagues, who can talk enlightened sexual politics all day long, then go out that night, and the next morning find themselves waking up in bed beside some flaming pig of a guy they can't for the life of them figure out how they ended up with. Thelma likes Carnes. That's pretty clear. And she gave a whole lot of herself away to him when she told him that story."

"So?"

"So anything can happen. They're on the way back to her place. Getting out of the car, he can ask her if he should tell the driver not to wait for him, he'll get a cab back. She might hear something in his voice, might see something in his face that persuades her she ought to let him come in with her."

I couldn't see how she was getting such notions from the conversation we'd just heard. She was not inclined to indulge herself in romantic fantasies. I was baffled by her. "So if you really want to know what happens, Marianne, go back over there and switch on the machine. We have the rest of this tape to listen to and even another one after that."

"No."

"What do you mean, 'No'?"

"We have to take it from here, Henry."

I had to think about that. I definitely had to think about that. I gave her a very quizzical look.

She stood up and switched off the lamp beside her chair.

XI

"Carnes wouldn't know how to respond if Thelma said, 'Yes, go ahead and let your driver go home,'" I told Marianne while she was arranging the pillows and bedcovers. I had already made myself comfortable on my side of the bed.

"Maybe Carnes has known all along that Thelma needs company just as much as he does." Marianne leaned over to turn her bedside light out, then settled herself in with her hip just touching mine. "Men don't usually know the difference between being horny and being lonely, but Carnes knew enough to ask you guys at the Project to find him some female companionship; so maybe he knows that if he waits for the right moment and says exactly the right thing in exactly the right tone of voice, it'll happen for them. She'll smile and look down and say, 'You can come in for a little while, Mr. Carnes.'"

"Ed."

Marianne laughed softly. "Ed."

"This is something you want to happen?"

She thought a moment. In spite of the dark, I thought she might have given me a small smile. "We're not necessarily talking sex here. I just don't want some silly obstacle denying them what they might be for each other."

"Like?"

"Like fear, pride, clumsiness, too much aggression on his part, too much caution on hers, asininity—"

"Bad timing?"

"Bad timing. Yes, certainly. You know how it is at the movies, Henry. You want the man and the woman to get together, to live happily."

"Even if you and your man have gotten together but not lived happily."

"Yes. Even if. Or if you and your woman have not lived happily, then maybe you're even more desperate about wanting it to happen for the movie couple. You want to walk out of that theater knowing that at least those people worked it out. If they got hold of what you don't have, then maybe it's at least worthwhile to keep on going with your life because eventually you might find the way for you and your sad old lady or your mean old man to take hold of it. You want to see it happen. *We* want to see it happen, don't we?"

"Yes," I said. "We want to see it happen. We're not talking sex, but we are talking biology, ontogeny recapitulating ontology, whatever." Then we were both quiet for a while, the two of us just lying beside each other and thinking to ourselves, before I went on. "So, let's just say Carnes does make it inside Thelma's front door? What happens next? How does it go?"

"You tell it, Henry."

"Why do I have to tell it?"

"There are two of us here, aren't there? I've gotten us from listening to the tape in the living room to lying here in the bed, talking with each other. You have no idea how much willpower that took. I can't go on. You take hold of the story. I'm exhausted."

"Amusing," I said, though I wasn't certain I understood her.

I decided to make the effort. It was cozy there with her, floating our voices up through the dark toward the ceiling. "Carnes comes in. They're standing there just inside the door. Thelma turns on some lights. He looks around. 'Nice,' he says. Meaning that he's intimidated by how tastefully she has furnished these rooms."

"So she glances back at her stereo," says Marianne, "and says, 'I'd put on some music, but I'd probably pick exactly what you'd hate to hear.' Meaning that he should relax, she has insecurities of her own."

"So Carnes would hear that in her voice," I say. "He'd hear that right off. He'd walk over and say, 'Let me pick something.' He'd immediately feel like he had a chance to be at ease with her."

"And she'd consider slipping off her heels, but then she'd have second thoughts about that, about maybe giving away too much too soon. So she'd keep her shoes on, but she'd ask him if he wanted anything to drink."

"He'd say, 'Tea, if you have it. Nothing if you don't.'"

"Yes. Yes. That's just the way he says things." Marianne's pleasure was such that my body could actually register it humming in her body beside me. "And of course Thelma's got a selection of teas that would keep the emperor of China happy. She tells him all the kinds of tea that she has."

"Which tickles him and makes him want to tease her."

"'What in the name of heaven are you going to do with all that tea, lady?' he'd say in that booming voice of his."

"And she'd blush a little in spite of herself."

"Yes, I expect she would."

"Have we seen her blush?"

"Well, we haven't, but we know what she'd look like anyway, don't we?"

"Yes, yes. All right. And does he blush? Does Carnes blush?"

"Seems unlikely, doesn't it? But he must do something. Obviously he gets embarrassed."

"Yes, he does."

"So she fixes tea, and he picks out a record. It's an old stereo. One of those big cratelike pieces of furniture like they used to sell at Sears. But it's in good shape. And she has plenty of records he's interested in. He picks a Sarah Vaughan that he knows has Miles playing the solos on."

"So the water's on, and the record starts. And Carnes is standing there in her living room. Thelma comes in and stands there, the two of them looking at each other and smiling, half out of politeness and half out of being pleased with themselves. So who says what next?"

"She does. She says, 'Sit down, Ed.'"

"And he's watching her eyes to see where she wants him to sit."

"It's the sofa."

"You're exactly right. It's the sofa."

Marianne and I are almost sitting up in the bed we're so wide awake. The story is humming right along. "They sit right down," I say.

XII

EDGAR CARNES, 61

Composer

Edgar DeWeese Carnes, a jazz musician whose compositions have recently come to be viewed as classics, died at his home yesterday, of an apparent heart attack. He was 61.

Born in Buffalo, New York, Mr. Carnes had resided in Chevy Chase, Maryland, for the past year and a half. After a number of years of residence in Göteborg, Sweden, Mr. Carnes had associated himself with the American Music Recovery Program sponsored by the National Endowment for the Arts in collaboration with the Smithsonian Institution. Among Mr. Carnes's notable compositions are "Scandinavian Suite," "Coldest Blues," "Hope in One Pocket," "Lady of Pain," and "Buffalo Stampede."

Eschewing the showmanship that brought so many of his peers into the public spotlight, Mr. Carnes, who was universally known as "Eddie," was considered primarily a musician's musician. The late Stan Getz said of him that his compositions were passionate, intricately conceived, deeply informed by both the jazz and classical traditions, and almost impossible to play well without the highest level of instrumental accomplishment.

Joe Henderson, a contemporary of Mr. Carnes's, spoke of their experience at the Village clubs in the mid-1960s: "When Eddie played those songs of his, there was a quality of revelation about them, as if he'd found something absolutely new between the cracks of what we were playing and writing in those days; he played his own pieces so sweetly they sounded familiar even though you'd never before heard them or anything quite like them."

Wynton Marsalis, a personal friend of the deceased, is currently producing a recording of Mr. Carnes's music that he hopes will enhance Mr. Carnes's reputation. "Eddie Carnes was an artist of absolute integrity," Mr. Marsalis said in a telephone interview this morning. "His songs were so advanced that you didn't know what you were hearing unless you had a good deal of musical education. Eddie wasn't trying to be ahead of his time; he just naturally was. And his playing was so intensely emotional that a lot of musicians backed away from it. But he seemed unaware of his public reputation—or the lack of it; he just played his horn and put together his tunes. Many of Eddie's pieces weren't even scored until recently, and these are tunes that people like Johnny Griffin and Sonny Stitt have been playing for years. Eddie Carnes was a one-of-a-kind jazzman, an example to all of us of somebody who never compromised his music."

Asked once why he had never played in the big bands that made the reputations of so many of his peers, Mr. Carnes explained, "My ears couldn't take in all those sounds at once. I tried sitting in a few times with the Clouds of Joy out in Kansas City. It felt like I had gone to the corner of hell they reserved especially for us jazzmen: I heard horns coming down out of the ceiling and coming up out of the floor. Only way I could stand it was by ingesting most of a fifth of Johnnie Walker. And then I couldn't read the charts, and nobody wanted me up on the stand anyway. I love every bit of Mr. Ellington's work, and I used to buy his records just as soon as they came out, but it still makes me nervous to listen to almost any other big band but his."

Henry McKernan, spokesperson for the National Endowment's Carnes Project, expressed "the sorrow and disappointment we all feel when the career of a major artist is unexpectedly cut short. Eddie Carnes was working right up until a few hours before he died. All of us here at the Project had grown immensely fond of the man. He was shy and considerate, a wonderful story-teller and late-night raconteur. It was a privilege being associated with Eddie Carnes. We're certain that his reputation will continue growing now that the Endowment and the Smithsonian can make his music more generally available than it has been. The truly sad part of it," Mr. McKernan explained, "is that Eddie had just recently begun moving in a new direction. We had all been excited listening to this new work and trying to anticipate where he was headed with it. We have enough of it on tape to know that it might have given him compositions of major consequence. As it is, we'll just have to guess what he might have done with this new material. He has left us more than enough to listen to and to appreciate for many years to come."

Mr. Carnes's first marriage, to Louise Campbell, also of Buffalo, New York, ended in a divorce. Their daughter, Constance, died in an auto accident in 1979. Mr. Carnes's second marriage, to Elizabeth Krönen, of Stockholm, Sweden, also ended in a divorce. He is survived by a brother, Dr. Ellis Carnes, of San Diego, California.

XIII

NATIONAL ENDOWMENT FOR THE ARTS

WASHINGTON, D.C. 20506

American Music Recovery Program

The Carnes Project

CONFIDENTIAL MEMORANDUM

David Huddle

Date: November 13, 1994

To: Robert Smallwood, Director
            The National Endowment for the Arts

From: Henry McKernan, Project Director
            American Music Recovery Program

Subject: The Future of the Carnes Project

Inasmuch as Mr. Carnes's death has unexpectedly altered the status of this project, our
discussion of its future must begin immediately.
Like every Project Director, I am intensely
aware of the pressure on you to justify each of
the Endowment's programs. An obvious response to
the death of Mr. Carnes, from the public, the
executive office, and the Congress, will be to
advocate wrapping up this project as soon as
possible. Therefore it is with special urgency
that I make this appeal to you to support my
request for extended funding of the Carnes
Project through the end of FY97.

Although it was clear from the beginning that
Mr. Carnes was an unacknowledged major figure in

the development of jazz from the mid-fifties through the late sixties, the Carnes Project has opened the possibility--and indeed now the *necessity*--of completely redefining his place in American music. Not only were we able to recover many of his unrecorded compositions from the seventies and eighties, we have also taken into our archives a virtual deluge of new material. Though this may be a somewhat exaggerated comparison, it is as if John Keats had been granted an additional five years of good health and ideal working conditions: the nature and scope of the achievement has been enlarged almost beyond our capacity to imagine it.

Ironically enough, by taking responsibility for Mr. Carnes's artistic life, the Endowment has implicitly accepted responsibility for Mr. Carnes's posterity. Had we not granted Mr. Carnes these months of being able to give maximum attention to his art, we would, to put it bluntly, have had a great deal less work to accomplish. As it is, we are now responsible for seeing to it that the history of American music gives Mr. Carnes his due place, a place that will be overwhelmingly informed by what he accomplished under our sponsorship.

We can only speculate about the final eval-
uation of Eddie Carnes's overall career, but the
unofficial consensus of those of us who have
worked on the Project is that the work of his
nineteen months with us is two or three times
more significant than what he accomplished in
the previous forty-some years of his working
life. By virtue of our work on the Carnes
Project, the Endowment can take pride in having
contributed significantly to the evolution of
American music. Though we should probably not
make any public claims to this effect, with
Eddie Carnes we actually succeeded in entering
the creative process of a major American artist.
Surely we can present these positive aspects of
our work in such a way as to enhance our funding possibilities for FY96 and FY97.

There being no precedent for the Carnes
Project, it is essential that the Endowment now
carry out a reckoning with what it actually means
for it (and us) to become intimately involved
with an individual artist. With Mr. Carnes, we
were able to observe and to record the daily life
of a creative genius working at the height of his

powers. We have the artist's shorthand notation
of a major composition, we have recordings of his
improvisational studies for that composition, we
have recordings of his ideas about the composition as he discussed them with other musicians.
We know whom he talked with and what advice those
persons offered. We know what Mr. Carnes ate for
lunch on the day he finished the piece, as well
as what music he listened to each evening as he
worked on it, what time he went to bed, and what
time he waked up. We even know whether or not he
shaved on the days when he composed its most
essential elements. The nature of artistic work
has never been so visible, has never been so
accessible to those of us who value it. The labor
of sorting through our archival materials and
carrying out the appropriate disposition of
recordings and documents has just begun. More
significantly, it is now possible for us to consider how the theoretical potential of this vast
body of material might be explored. What can
these documents and recordings tell us about
creativity? About genius? About inspiration? In
processing the Carnes materials, we may find
that we must function as scientists and artists

as well as librarians.

We officers of the Endowment must also begin to address certain unanticipated issues related to sponsoring and studying artistic endeavor. In our initial planning stages, we gave a great deal of discussion to the matter of Mr. Carnes's personal well-being. I take some pride in knowing that we did everything possible to make him feel at home here at Project Headquarters. We have every reason to believe that his last months were among the happiest of Mr. Carnes's life. The exuberance and wit of his last compositions and recordings will testify to his high spirits during his final days.

However, another "personal" dimension of this project must also be considered in our deliberations over the future of the American Music Recovery Program--the personal lives of our own officers. To set it forth candidly, my own private life has been severely altered because of my emotional involvement with Mr. Carnes and his music. Eddie Carnes's death has plunged me more deeply than ever into the work of the Project. At the suggestion of my wife, I've taken an apartment within walking distance of Project

Headquarters, and though I find this arrangement convenient, I am somewhat dismayed at the extent to which the Project has taken over my life.

Some months ago, I had a dream in which I served as Carnes's translator; although the dream was absurd in most respects, I believe it accurately signaled a kind of responsibility that has settled upon me as a result of my directing the Carnes Project. Whether or not I am the right person to be his "translator" is beside the point--and one of the most troubling things my wife said to me in our last conversation was that Eddie Carnes never intended his music for bureaucrats like me. Whether or not that's true, I am the person responsible for delivering to the world what Eddie Carnes had to say to it in the final months of his life. I have accepted that assignment.

A lesson I have taken from Mr. Carnes is that you have to, as he put it, "take what comes to you and go with it." Eddie Carnes came into my life. He came into it much more profoundly than I ever intended for him to do so. Although he was a man whose experience was utterly different from mine, knowing him as I came to know him was a rare privilege. I have no choice now but to "go with it."

I know that matters of funding beyond the immediate fiscal year are problematic, but I will be greatly reassured if I can know that I have your support in my request to sustain the Carnes Project at least through FY97. I must point out that perverse as it may seem, Carnes's death offers us an opportunity for rallying support for the Project. The occasion has brought forth attention from the media, and it has focused sentiment in the jazz community. Relevant, too, is the familiar phenomenon of living artists who are largely ignored by the public but who become both popular and important after their deaths. Timing is crucial, and this may be the ideal time to request extended funding for the Carnes Project. Should you need further information or assistance from me in drafting up the documents to support our request, please contact me immediately. I'm eager to help in any way possible, and I'm available to you at almost any hour of the day.

Many thanks for your consideration of this request. I look forward to receiving your timely reply.

XIV

I HAVE VERY LITTLE right to speak about Ed Carnes. My acquaintance with the man was extremely limited. We met at a party; we talked a while; we enjoyed each other's company sufficiently for him to extend an invitation to me to have an evening out with him and for me to accept his invitation. We had a very pleasant dinner, during which we exchanged stories of our childhoods, our growing up.

As you might imagine, our lives were very different—though perhaps that difference was more of an opportunity than it was an obstacle to our friendship.

I was intrigued with Mr. Carnes; I "liked" him—as my students would put it. I wished to see more of him. And my sense of Ed Carnes was one of his trying to journey toward me. On both occasions when I was with him, I had the impression that he was making an effort to find out about me, to understand me, to see the world from my point of view, to be close to me.

In the one evening we spent in each other's company, when I asked him to speak about himself, he obliged me with such candidness that I could hardly help but be touched by him. And so I responded by speaking to him as openly as I possibly could about my own childhood and growing up. I surprised myself with what I was willing to tell him—though perhaps I saw it as a more significant revelation than he did. At any rate, I would say that he and I had a meaningful exchange of—what should I call it?—personal information about each other.

So there's that: Ed Carnes was willing to try to become close to another person—and from my limited experience, I'd say that's a rare quality in a man.

After he had taken me out for dinner, and we'd gotten into that car that the Endowment provided for him, Ed gave me a mischievous look and asked if I would mind if we stopped by a little club where some friends of his were playing. He explained that he had not been in a club for a number of years and that until now he'd been afraid to enter one again because of his drinking. He knew that in that atmosphere the temptation to drink would be too much for him. But he thought that my being with him that night would protect him.

If I had said no, I'm certain that he'd have understood. After all, I had been under the impression that our evening was nearly over. He knew that I was ready to go home, say thank you and good night to him. He knew that I was tired and that I had had an exhausting week at school. But he was asking me to do something for him, something that was important to him. I wanted him to know that I cared that much about him. I said all right, I could probably stay out another hour or so and not fall asleep on him.

So he had his driver take us to Blues Alley, where David Murray was playing with some other musicians; Marcus Roberts was the young man playing piano—Ed was very excited about him. I don't remember the others.

From the car to the door of Blues Alley, holding onto Ed's arm, I had a reassuring sense of being with him, being close to him. Once we were inside the door of that place, with that beery smell and all that noise and smoke, I felt him just drift away from me. I withdrew my hand from his arm very soon after we were inside, but I don't think he noticed. He reminded me of some of my students who can be very attentive in my classroom but who become completely different human beings once they step out into that hallway.

Of course Ed was welcomed like a long-lost brother by the musicians who saw him come in. It wasn't more than a half hour before they sent his driver back outside to bring in Ed's saxophone, which just happened to be in the trunk of the car. I wondered if he hadn't deliberately set me up for this situation. Apparently, he had hoped I'd agree to go with him to Blues Alley, and apparently he had hoped he would be invited to play with the band. Though he wasn't entirely innocent, he also wasn't guilty of outright trickery either.

Excitement just spread through the whole place when they started whispering, "Eddie Carnes is going to play with the band." I felt it all around me—by that time we were sitting at a table where his friends had made room for us. I no longer felt on equal footing with him, but I was still in touch with Ed enough to know that he was very excited, too, in spite of his efforts to sit there nonchalantly.

He walked up to the bandstand, unpacked and assembled his instrument, then sat down and gave me a steady look that I think he meant to convey that he intended this occasion to be a kind of present to me, a gift. It took quite a bit of concentration for me to understand his intentions because even if he had been Duke Ellington himself, returned from the dead, I wouldn't have wanted to hear him play in such a noisy, bad-smelling place at that hour of the night. I could hardly catch my breath for the smoke. There was so much noise that the only way you could communicate with anyone was by screaming into his or her ear. But this was something Ed was doing for me. I tried chanting it to myself as I sat there among the many people who worshipped him: Ed Carnes is doing this for me.

When they started playing, the crowd quieted down immediately. Even I felt a shiver of anticipation, or maybe just nervousness, pass through me. They had chosen a very bluesy tune—one of Ed's compositions, I think—which they played so slowly, it was almost a ballad. Then Ed stood up to take his solo at the microphone.

At that moment I divided into two separate people. Part of me felt the intensity and the delicacy of his playing—and I really could perceive a beauty coming out of his horn that I had never before experienced, what I would prefer to call a *glory* of sound, except that I doubt Ed would have liked such a spiritual word for the earthy way he was playing.

The other part of me was just objectively witnessing the whole performance. That part of me was seeing a man who was forever out of my reach—a man who *had* to remain distant from me because that person existed only when he was playing his saxophone.

I'd say this other—disengaged—part of me was cold and calculating except that this is also the part of me that had tears coming to my eyes. Because that *judging* part of myself was making me understand what I was hearing: Ed Carnes was calling to me, asking me so very sweetly to come to him. To come to him there in the song. To *stay* there with him in the song.

At the same time, his playing was telling me, You can never be here with me, you can never touch me here in this song, this is mine and mine alone.

While I was sitting there at his table with his friends and admirers, listening to his music, this question came to me: What can you do with a man like that?

The answer came, too, very quickly: Nothing.

I had no choice. It was as if someone had opened up a door on a long, empty hallway that led into deeper and deeper darkness and then asked me if I wanted to enter. My answer was just so clearly, so overwhelmingly *no!*—I had to stand up from that table. I had to leave that place.

Of course I made my manners as best I could. I explained to Ed's friends that I wasn't feeling well, that rather than interrupt him in the middle of something that obviously meant a great deal to him, I would call a cab and go home on my own. I assured everyone that I would be fine.

My friends tell me I am not a worldly person. Perhaps if I had been more accustomed to the world of music—of jazz, of Blues Alley—I might not have been such a coward in the face of what I understood about Ed Carnes. I might have had the courage to enter that dark hallway, or I might have loved his music so much that I would have been willing to struggle futilely for the rest of my life—or the rest of his—to be close to him.

Regret was what gave me my last glimpse of Ed. I had been thinking to myself, Why can't you be the kind of person who can be here for him? All he wants is for you to be here for him.

As I made my way back through that crowd of drinkers and jazz fans at Blues Alley, I had been chiding myself, How can you be so prideful as to walk away from this man?

Just before I walked out to the coatroom, I turned to see if Ed was noticing that I was leaving. He wasn't. He was standing up there at the microphone with sweat broken out all across his forehead and his forehead wrinkled up into these deep lines with his eyes squeezed shut. Just for the moment of my seeing him like that, I thought that his saxophone looked like an instrument of torture that had been attached—against his will—to his poor mouth. He seemed to be straining to push it away from himself.

The effort Ed was making to produce that gorgeous sound was perfectly visible on his face. The music his horn was playing was telling the world how much he longed to be close to some-body—but his eyes were shut! They were shut so tightly that he couldn't possibly have seen another human being, even one who might have been standing close enough to breathe on him, let alone one who was all the way across a room full of people, waving her hand at him, trying to tell him good-bye.